Moonwind

Moon

wind

Louise Lawrence

1 8 ⚑ 1 7

HARPER & ROW, PUBLISHERS

Cambridge, Philadelphia, San Francisco, London, Mexico City, São Paolo, Singapore, Sydney

NEW YORK

Designed by Joyce Hopkins
1 2 3 4 5 6 7 8 9 10
First American Edition

Library of Congress Cataloging-in-Publication Data
Lawrence, Louise, 1943–
  Moonwind.

  Summary: One of two teenage winners of a trip to
earth's first lunar base falls in love with an astral
extraterrestrial who has been stranded on the moon for
thousands of years and who needs his help to repair her
spaceship so that she can return home.
  [1. Science fiction] I. Title.
PZ7.L4367Mo 1986   [Fic]   85-45507
ISBN 0-06-023733-3
ISBN 0-06-023734-1 (lib. bdg.)

For Margaret Clark,
who provided a new beginning

Moonwind

1

She dreamed.

And the ship voice called her.

"Wake up, Bethkahn!"

She opened her eyes. Light in the cryogenic chamber was dim blue, and when she turned her head she could see through the transparent dome that covered her . . . curved silver walls and empty sleeping berths, a doorway leading into loneliness. She was the only one alive on a dead uncharted world, and she could not bear it. The ship knew that and should not have woken her.

"What do you want?" she asked angrily.

The ship voice hesitated before replying.

Then it told her.

"We are no longer alone here, mistress."

Bethkahn lay unmoving, not daring to believe, yet

believing anyway in spite of herself. The ship would not lie to her. Rondahl had returned . . . Mahna had returned . . . the whole crew had returned. Elation filled her, and all she had suffered seemed silly now that it was over. She wanted to leap from her berth, laugh and sing, rush wild through the blue-silver spaces to greet them. But she had been trained at the Galactic Academy and was no longer a child. She was a junior technician aboard an explorer-class starship, and Rondahl would expect her to behave as one. But joy and relief spilled over as tears, and she grinned stupidly, cried stupidly, not caring that the ship was watching her.

The ship had seen emotion before. At first she had had to tell it how she felt and why. But then it had learned to recognize cause and effect, and although it could never share her feelings it seemed to understand. Through her fear and panic, desperation and despair, it had done its best to comfort her. Now, seeing tears and smiles, its voice stayed silent, allowed her some moments to herself.

"How long have I been sleeping?" she asked it.

"Ten thousand orbital years," it replied.

She could not take it in. Ten thousand years was too long to imagine. Time in the cryogenic chamber had been suspended with her life, centuries compressed into seconds. It was as if she had slept and woken a moment later exactly as she was, untouched by age or experience. She laughed with the sheer joy of it, and her thoughts turned back to the beginning.

*　　*　　*

4

A faulty stabilizer, Rondahl had said, as the ship spun sickeningly through pulsing dimensions of time and space. And spinning still, it had slowed to sublight speed, emerged among unknown suns in a remote arm of a spiral galaxy. They had landed on the attendant moon of an unknown planet to make repairs. To Rondahl it had seemed a bonus, that turquoise blue world turning in the black sky over them. Jewel-bright and beautiful, it was waiting to be explored. The whole crew had gone there, and Bethkahn had watched them leave—a fleet of tiny survey craft, their wings catching the light, speeding over the crater rim to vanish among the stars. And she, being the junior technician, remained behind. She had to mend the stabilizer, Rondahl had said.

At first she had not really minded. Perhaps she had even been glad. Fresh from the Academy, an inexperienced girl on her initiation flight, it had not been easy. Mahna had been kind to her, but Rondahl had seen her as a nuisance, and the senior technicians had given her all the boring routine jobs to do. Adjusting the stabilizer was just one more. She had to remove the wall panel and crawl on her stomach through the flight control conduits.

The ship voice had guided her. Usually it spoke only to Rondahl and Mahna, who were in charge of it, but with Bethkahn alone on board she became its mistress. It had been a wonderful, awesome experience having the whole vast starship working for her and responding to her presence. It had given her a feeling of freedom and power, and she had reveled in her solitude. She could command it to speak or be silent. She could draw on the knowledge contained in its computer mind. There was a fault, it said, in number three stabilizer. Bethkahn found it blown, two metal blades sheared off under pressure and the whole stabilizing unit needing to be replaced. But when she checked the storeroom she discovered they had run out of spares. She could have made a laser weld, but the power packs were all on empty. It was then Bethkahn realized they were in trouble.

"What shall I do?" she had asked the ship. "We can't take off without a stabilizer!"

"That's Rondahl's problem," it informed her. "You must leave it for him. He took the risk, and I told him repeatedly I was due for an overhaul, advised him to return to base. But he paid me no heed. There's nothing you can do, Bethkahn."

So Bethkahn had learned that Rondahl the ship master was not perfect, and she waited nervously for his return. Suddenly time had assumed a meaning. She grew aware of its passing and needed to measure it. But the ship had nothing to go by. Parsecs and megaparsecs could not apply. They had to work it out by planetary motion, the moon and its world revolving around the nearby star. They had counted in moondays—one . . . two . . . three . . . eye blinks in eternity. But Bethkahn, trapped in one space-time dimension, experienced its slowness. Solitude changed to loneliness, and although the ship voice kept her company it was not the same as having the crew around.

Rooms and corridors oppressed her with their silences. She missed Mahna's laughter and Rondahl's frown. But down on the planet's surface they were absorbed in their survey and did not notice time. Bethkahn waited and waited. Half of one orbital year was nothing, the ship voice had said.

Eventually she tried the transmitter, but no one answered her. Lost on that blue, bright world beneath its swirling atmosphere, she supposed, they did not hear. She dispatched the last long-range scanner. But the survey craft were hidden by drifts of white cloud, and the life traces of the crew were indistinguishable among millions of other life traces. The planet teemed with primordial existences, and neither Bethkahn nor the ship could identify the ones they knew. And when the probe burned up during a volcanic eruption, her anxiety turned to panic.

The planet was geologically unstable, and Rondahl might never return. Bethkahn might be trapped forever in a crippled starship far from the main flight paths. She would not listen to the ship voice trying to calm her. She transmitted a general distress call across the galaxy, transmitted and transmitted until the delicate circuitry fused and was useless. Then she could do nothing else but wait . . . through moondays blinding white and long airless nights, years turning to decades. How long her messages would take to reach the starbases only the ship could compute, but it would be thousands of years, it had said, before help would arrive. And then

7

who would hear her? Her voice crying through a dead transmitter? Or see the starship buried in moondust under a millennium of time?

For her mistake Bethkahn had blamed the ship. She had screamed in her isolation and despair, beat with clenched fists on its cold curved walls, hating everything it was—an unfeeling machine, a jail of white light, a useless metal artifact that could do nothing to help.

Through years of madness she had gone outside and searched the moon's barren surface, looking for someone who would love her, arms that would hold her, another living being to comfort her and care. But nothing lived on its pock-marked surface. Nothing moved among its mountains and craters and oceans of dust.

The ship was all that remained for Bethkahn, her only sanctuary, her only friend. Again and again she returned to it, sobbed out her heart in its silver-white halls, told it how she felt. She had said she would rather die than live through an eternity of loneliness and asked it to destroy her. But the ship was programmed to preserve the lives of its crew. One day Rondahl would return, it said, and instead of death it offered her sleep and forgetfulness, an escape route of dreams in the cryogenic chamber. But now it had woken her. It said she was not alone anymore, that Rondahl and Mahna were back. Or maybe it had not said that?

Her senses sharpened. The last traces of sleep fled from her head, and she pressed the button. The transparent dome of her sleeping berth raised automatically, and automatically the blue light brightened to white.

Curved silver walls glowed with reflected radiance. Bethkahn sat up. She could hear the silence and sense the almighty emptiness stretching away.

"What do you mean?" she screamed. "There's no one here! Where are they?"

"Outside," said the ship. "They are outside, Bethkahn. And they are not who you think. They are not Rondahl or Mahna or anyone else we know."

"You mean we are being rescued?"

The ship sighed deeply.

"Not exactly," it said.

2

Bethkahn pulled on a shimmering suit, waistcoat and trousers that flared and folded and clung to her shape, insubstantial as light. Gold and vermilion the fire colors flickered, moved as she moved through silver curving corridors toward the main console room. A thousand questions flittered mothlike through her head. The ship was agitated, adding to her confusion, hinting at things that did not make sense, and evading the facts.

"So what exactly are you telling me?" Bethkahn asked. "If they have not come from the star worlds to rescue us, then where have they come from? Who are they?"

"They have come from the planet," the ship voice said.

"But they have nothing to do with Rondahl?"

"They have everything to do with Rondahl, mistress. That is what I am trying to tell you. The life-trace comparisons are unmistakable. Each one is individually different, but each one shows a degree of similarity to various members of our crew that is too great to be coincidence. These beings who have come to this moon are familial, Bethkahn. They are related."

"That's ridiculous!" Bethkahn told it. "How can they be? You must be mistaken."

A door slid open before her, revealing the great dark astrodome dotted with electronic stars, quadrants of the galaxy charted and explored, and the multicolored tracks of the main flight paths. Home world was a speck of green light, Khio Three distant and unreachable, disturbing a longing that was instantly suppressed. Bethkahn mounted the central dais, seated herself in the silver chair where once Rondahl had sat. She was unqualified and had no right to it, but the ship called her "mistress" and functioned for her benefit—every wire and circuit in its mechanized body, every thought in its computer brain. Now her slim fingers threw the switches, bringing its dozen blank vision screens to life.

She ran a life-trace comparison for herself, trying to match the psychic energy patterns of the original crew to those who had recently come here, overlaying peaks and troughs, noting the incidence of identity. The ship voice was right. The similarities were undeniable. They were kindred souls, and Bethkahn could offer no dispute. This one was related to Rondahl. This one to Keirharah. This one to Dahn . . . Dahn, with his blue eyes, who had once gazed at her in love. Bethkahn bit her lip and looked away, feeling the anguish inside her,

11

not knowing how to bear the implications. She could see the ghost of her own face mirrored in the blank vision screen beside her, a girl with coal-black hair and garments of fire.

"They have bred," she said dully.

"That is the logical conclusion," said the ship.

"But why?" wailed Bethkahn. "I don't understand! How could they stay there, and breed, and leave me here? How could they abandon this mission? How could they? Why should they? It doesn't make sense!"

The great ship sighed, sound echoing through its halls, imitating emotion. For ten thousand years it had protected Bethkahn from the knowledge, keeping it from her, not wanting to destroy the only hope she had. But now it had no choice. Its safety was threatened and it had to tell her the truth.

"Ten thousand years is a long time," the ship voice murmured. "And there is something I have not told you, mistress. Before Rondahl departed for the planet he sent out a probe scanner. It landed on an oceanic island and relayed the surface conditions. Believing it safe, the survey ships followed. I monitored them, of course. I monitored the seismic tremors and saw them destroyed. The island continent sank beneath the sea a few planetary days after touchdown."

In the long silence Bethkahn neither moved nor spoke.

"Rondahl was stranded," the ship voice said sadly.

"And you let me go on believing . . ."

"I let you hope," the ship voice corrected.

"You lied to me!" Bethkahn said harshly.

12

"No," said the ship. "I merely concealed the facts. Having worked with Rondahl through eons of light years it was worth saying nothing. There was always a chance he would find a way."

"What chance?" Bethkahn said angrily. "There was no way he, or any of them, could escape from a primitive world without building some kind of replacement craft. And that's not like replacing a blown stabilizer! Physical tasks need physical bodies! And we don't have physical bodies! We have astral bodies! The only power we have is the power of our minds, and there are limits as to how much minds can influence matter. It takes a body of flesh to refine raw metal, forge component parts, assemble a ship! There was never any hope for them!"

"Not unless they entered flesh," agreed the ship.

Bethkahn considered it. It was a common enough practice—a way of exploring, experiencing, and gleaning information from the various worlds they surveyed. She had been in flesh herself, briefly, during a landfall on the fifth planet of Bahtoomi's star. Stepping from the landing craft she had seen lake water lapping on a pebbly shore, rose-gold, reflecting the light of a red giant sun in a pure pink sky. Dark birds wheeled and screamed above crimson reed beds, and a faint musty fungoid scent drifted on the wind from the forest of red-leaved trees behind her. They had moved among mulberry shadows and come to the lakeside to drink, Bahtoomi's deer with their mottled plum-colored pelts, spiraling horns, and velvet black eyes. Bethkahn would have been content merely to watch them, content with her own sense perceptions, but Mahna had told her to enter one and become enfleshed.

Often, as a child on Khio Three, she had been one with trees and flowers, her spirit absorbed by the natural forms around her. But Bahtoomi's deer were alien and wild, sentient creatures with souls of their own, and Bethkahn had been reluctant, almost afraid. Then she felt warmth and heartbeats, the power of muscle and sinew, heard lake water ripple and leaf rustle and bird cry, smelled a thousand separate scents. Ears pricked and nostrils flared. One scent, one sound triggered a sweet sharp thrill of alarm, and the body responded, bounded away, leaped through fern brake into forest and sped through the red crimson flickering of shadows and light.

What Bahtoomi's deer had feared was instantly forgotten. It had neither memory nor imagination, and Bethkahn, sharing its sensations, sharing its skin, could not even guess. Its motivation had changed to hunger, and it browsed with the herd on mushrooms that tasted of bonemeal . . . until death fell on it from above. Bethkahn felt claws tearing flesh, felt pain and terror, smelled blood, saw cat eyes glitter, and heard an animal snarl. And the cry was hers when its fanged teeth ripped the deer's throat. She had fled, sobbing, back to the survey craft and never wanted to be enfleshed again.

But Mahna had found her, made her become a bird to overcome her fear . . . a sky hawk riding the windy air, to hover, plunge groundward, and kill. Talons curled and clutched, and a small life ended. Bethkahn ripped and fed, knowing the hunger of the hunter, its joy in the hot taste of her prey. In flesh she had killed and been killed, experiences alien to her nature, not easy to understand. Flesh was never easy, Mahna had said. It was cruel always, a mixture of violence and beauty, bittersweet feelings that were difficult to bear. Their kind seldom stayed enfleshed for long. They experienced it briefly and were glad to be free.

But the ship voice suggested . . .

"It was a primitive world," Bethkahn repeated. "It showed no signs of civilization, no indication of life forms advanced enough to understand intricate instructions or build complicated machinery. Even if the crew had entered flesh, even if they had found a suitable species, they would have needed to establish an evolutionary program, and that would have taken them thousands of years. . . ."

Bethkahn stopped talking.

Suddenly she understood.

"Are you saying this is what they have done?"

"It seems a logical hypothesis," said the ship.

There had been evolutionary programs before in other parts of the galaxy. Bethkahn had learned of them at the Academy—transcendent worlds where flesh was made beautiful by the spirit that inhabited it. Some volunteered for it, saw it as a challenge, a way of gaining individual understanding. And flesh had its advantages. It was a mind-body combination that had built this ship, set Bethkahn and others of her kind free to travel the universe.

She knew the theory. It was spiritual possession. Not the temporary sharing of a host creature's body, as she had done with Bahtoomi's deer, but permanent, throughout its lifetime, the controversial eviction of its soul. Those from the stars, encased in flesh, mated with those of the chosen planet, engendering hybrid children. And when the body died, they entered another, were born again, reincarnating over and over and repeating the process of interbreeding, their spirits mingling and strengthening and reinforcing the original strain. Each new generation of children became increasingly accomplished, increasingly advanced—apes evolving to angels in a few thousand years.

But for those involved there were risks attached. If the spirit was not strong enough, flesh could become dominant, the mind obsessed with the body it inhabited. Souls could degenerate, turn hedonistic, renegade, or bad. Trapped within flesh a soul could lose sight of its origin and purpose, even lose sight of itself. Those involved needed guidance and monitoring, galactic counseling and spiritual help in times of trouble. It was madness to think of initiating an evolutionary program on an unknown planet without off-world supervision.

"Rondahl wouldn't do it," Bethkahn said.

"I think he has already done it," said the ship.

"He would never risk it. None of them would!"

"But those outside are their descendents," said the ship. "We cannot deny it, Bethkahn. They have come from the same planet. Their life traces show too many exact matches to be explained in any other way. These souls bound in flesh are Rondahl's solution, and I do not like them. They must not discover us, mistress. They must never discover us here."

3

Bethkahn stared at the vision screen, at the pale life-trace flicker of an unknown being. It was flesh bound and fleeting, having no memory of Khio Three, its link with the stars, inheriting only some vague indefinable sensing, an ancestral instinct that was driving it toward them. It had come to this moon as a step on the way and was unaware of her, not knowing her plight. And the joy of Bethkahn's waking was gone to despair as the long-ago loneliness reached out toward her, disturbing a terror and longing from which she could not escape. Rondahl's descendents were not to be trusted, the ship voice had said.

"I want to see them," Bethkahn said fearfully.

Time flickered on the vision screen, sequential events that the ship had recorded and of which Bethkahn had been unaware. Her long-ago distress signal brought a response. Rescue ships came and continued to come—freight carriers, star cruisers, exploration vessels from every corner of the universe. But each one headed for the planet, lured by the bright blue shimmer of sunlight on water, its swirling atmosphere, its myriad indications of life. They paid no heed to a dead moon where Bethkahn had been sleeping, although the ship had done its best to attract attention. Again and again it had sent out the short-range scanners, their small power jets whirling up the dust of dry lunar seas, trailing gray walls of mist across the desert landscape. A dozen tiny transmitters bleeped messages that were never heard, radiophonic voices feeble as gnat whines dissolving among the stars. At other times the ship had activated its main drive units, blown itself free of dust and debris until the crater smoked like a great volcano. But no one noticed and no ship landed . . . until the Earth beings came.

"Earth?" said Bethkahn.

"Their name for the planet," said the ship.

"They do not use the galactic tongue?"

"Either they have not been taught it or it has degenerated and become unrecognizable," the ship voice replied. "I have compiled vocabularies of two principal languages."

"So they are two different species?"

"They are all one species," said the ship. "But there are many tribes, many subdivisions, many cultures, rituals, and languages. There are superficial variations among the main ethnic groups, but the biological infrastructure . . ."

"Just show me," Bethkahn interrupted.

It was Earth year 1969, and there was the flesh of which the ship voice had spoken, the first tentative arrivals—two grotesque humanoid shapes, helmeted and faceless, emerging from an equally grotesque lunar module. A voice gabbled words which the ship voice translated. "This is a giant leap forward for mankind." Through the eyes of a scanner Bethkahn stared at them—space-suited bipeds lumbering around on the Moon's barren surface, leaving their footprints in the dust and planting their flag. She had wanted to love Rondahl's descendents. She had wanted to rush outside and welcome them. But she could not feel kinship for those alien primate things. Her whole being shrank from them, and tears prickled her eyes.

"He has failed," she whispered. "Rondahl has failed. Those are not advanced evolutionary beings. They are subhuman! Cavorting imbecilic monsters!"

"They have reached their moon," the ship reminded her.

Bethkahn shuddered.

"I'm going back to the cryogenic chamber," she said.

"You can't do that!" the ship said urgently. "I need you, Bethkahn. Those earth creatures are dangerous, mistress! They threaten us!"

Bethkahn stayed, watched in alarm as the ship continued to replay the last long century of time—a succession of lunar landings and bloated humanoid forms who remained for a few hours and then departed. Red, white, and blue, their starred-and-striped banners hung motionless through succeeding decades of silence.

But then, fifty years later, the Earth beings returned. From the rim of the crater high in the mountains, a single scanner watched their spaceships arrive, a fleet of sleek transporters bringing in people and supplies. Unseen in the distance it recorded the building of their moonbase, an underground complex and prefabricated buildings rising from the dust. Technologically they had advanced beyond belief. Gone were the cumbersome space suits they had worn before. Bethkahn saw slim limbs clad in silver fabric, saw grace in their movements, a familiarity of form that no longer repelled. Their domed helmets showed no facial features but only reflections, yet she relaxed as she watched them and smiled in her relief.

They were not monsters. They were lithe as Bahtoomi's hunting cats and surefooted as the dancers on Aravis Nine. And how many times had Mahna told her not to judge life by appearances alone? But the ship voice had said they were dangerous. Bethkahn studied them warily, their sleek ships landing and departing, their wheeled machines fanning out across the Moon's surface. There were close to a thousand flesh-and-blood beings living and working within the sealed environment of the American base, the ship voice informed her. More manned the remote outposts, and far to the north the Russians had established a similar base. Russian and American—one species, two tribes. Bright points of light on the video display map showed their whereabouts.

"Sinus Iridum . . . Mare Vaporum," the ship voice said.

Haltingly Bethkahn repeated the names, meaningless syllables of an unfamiliar language, words sounding strange on her tongue. Bay of Rainbows, Sea of Mists, the ship voice translated. Strange misnomers, but they made the bleak moon seem suddenly beautiful, an alien dreamlike world. What kind of minds culled mists and rainbows from barren deserts of dust? What kind of beings had Rondahl's descendents become? And why were they dangerous?

"Give me an infrastructure scan," Bethkahn said quietly.

"Screen three," said the ship.

Bethkahn pressed the button, and the form appeared—bone structure fleshed in white light. It was not some grotesque parody of herself. It was a physical replica, a flesh-and-blood body molding to the spirit that inhabited it, a being bred in Rondahl's own image. Delight shone from her eyes. Such knowledge changed everything. She was no longer alone on a dead, uncharted world. She had only to walk to the moonbase and hold out her hand.

"These beings are beautiful!" she said.

"They are flesh," said the ship.

"I can talk with them . . . laugh with them . . ."

"Predators," said the ship. "They prey on other life forms and kill one another."

Bethkahn shrugged.

"Flesh has to eat," she said.

"But they commit murder," said the ship.

"Murder?" said Bethkahn. "What do you mean?"

The ship seemed to pause before replying, its presence hovering in the white light on the edges of her vision, an impression of entity that was gone when she turned her head. Many times in the past Bethkahn had been deceived into believing the ship was alive. It was an illusion born out of loneliness, for it simply existed mechanically and was all around her—in the curved walls of the main console room, in the astrodome stars and the navigational computers, in the manufactured circuits of its mind. It was a thing of logic, not capable of making moral judgments, but it came very close to judging the Earth beings now.

"What do you mean?" Bethkahn repeated.

"Flesh can corrupt," the ship voice said. "It can subordinate the spirit within it. They are not beautiful, Bethkahn, nor is their world. Their communications tell me . . . terrible things take place on it—war and famine, cruelty and monstrous acts of destruction. I fear what will happen if they should discover us. I am afraid, Bethkahn."

Bethkahn stared unseeingly at the shape on the vision screen—bones fleshed in light, a living being, beautiful, dangerous. Flesh was never easy, Mahna had said. It was cruel always, and Bethkahn could not forgive. She could forgive a predator that killed to live, but not an intelligence that murdered life, a spirit that did not care.

"I am afraid!" the ship voice repeated.

"You are a machine!" Bethkahn said harshly. "You

cannot feel fear. And I am immaterial, so they can do nothing to me. I'm going back to the cryogenic chamber, and whatever else happens I don't want to know!"

"Mistress!" squawked the ship. "You have to help me, mistress! They could break into me, take me to pieces, or blow me up! If I am destroyed who then will care for you? Think of it, Bethkahn! Think of it! You can't let that happen! You cannot ignore them and hide away. You have to mend my stabilizer as soon as possible and let me take you home!"

He dreamed.

And Karen called him.

"Hey Gary! Wake up!"

She switched on the light, and Gareth squinted into the sudden brightness. She was wearing a lurid green jump suit, and the room was painted white, spartanly furnished, and small as a clothes closet, with a washbasin and a single chair. Window blinds sealed out the view, and in the alcove opposite his bed a blank computer screen reflected his face. He had a headache from last night's reception, and Karen had no right to come barging into his room.

"What do you want?" he asked irritably.

"Drew's waiting to see you in his office."

"Who the hell's Drew?"

"Drew Steadman, the base medic. You met him last

25

night, remember? The tall guy with red hair? He and Commander Bradbury will be showing us around after breakfast, but first you have to have a medical check."

"I had one before we left," Gareth muttered.

"It's only routine," said Karen. "Pulse rate and blood pressure, that kind of thing. I guess he just wants to make sure we've survived the journey okay. This place is fantastic, Gary, it really is. I can't wait to see it."

The room reminded Gareth of a cheap motel, stark and impersonal except for his travel bag lying unpacked on the floor. It offered no clue as to where he was. And Karen's loud American drawl and the green of her jump suit made his headache worse. Pain thumped with the light behind his eyes. He rolled over and pulled the bedspread up around his ears.

"Don't go back to sleep!" said Karen. "You'll miss the sunrise, and Drew says it only happens once every twenty-eight days. If you turn left at the end of the corridor his office is the third door on the right. Shall I open your window blinds?"

"Let 'em alone!" growled Gareth.

"Are you always so grouchy first thing in the morning?"

"You never heard of a hangover, girlie?"

Karen laughed.

"There's ham and eggs and waffles for breakfast," she informed him. "And they stop serving at nine. Better ask Drew to give you some Alka-Seltzer. I'll be waiting for you in the cafeteria in half an hour."

"Make it forty minutes," Gareth said.

"I don't know how you can lie there anyway. We're on the Moon, for Christ's sake, and you're wasting time! How can you lie in bed, Gary?"

"Because you're in my flaming room and I've got nothing on!" Gareth told her.

She left, finally, returned to her own room to put a new roll of film in her camera, her presence lingering in the smell of her perfume and chewing gum. Gareth dressed in jeans and a sweatshirt and weighted canvas shoes, ran a hand through his hair, and made his way to the base medic's office. A man in a white coat opened the door to him.

"Doctor Steadman?"

"Drew," said the base medic. "You feel okay?"

"I've a headache," said Gareth.

"You also have your sweatshirt on backward."

Gareth had no recollection of having met Drew Steadman during last night's reception, but he liked him immediately—a tall, red-haired, friendly American. Unlike Karen, Drew was quiet and soft-spoken, easy to talk to and willing to listen. He had graduated in space psychology and had been on the Moon for almost three years. He gave Gareth a glass of fizzing liquid that made him belch, a pill for his headache, and a quick physical checkup.

"Welsh?" he said.

"That's right," said Gareth. "The first Welshman on the Moon. Put my shirt on, can I?"

"You can," said Drew. "And don't forget the dragon goes in front."

27

Gareth waited, soothed by the room's stillness as Drew filled in details in his file. It was dark outside, the moonbase a sprawl of lighted buildings nestling near the foot of the Lunar Apennines in the Mare Vaporum, Sea of Mists. Solar panels gleamed silver in the starlight, and great telescopic dishes marched away over the sharply curving horizon. The roadway and launch pads were smooth scars in the dust. Inside, the air-conditioning hummed softly and a pot of geraniums bloomed coral pink on the filing cabinet.

"So how does it feel?" Drew asked at last.

"Unreal," said Gareth. "As if any moment now I'm going to wake up and find myself back on Earth. I can't believe I'm here!"

Drew smiled.

"Some prize, a trip to the Moon. You're here all right—where science and religion finally meet."

"You read my essay?"

" 'The Lunacy Syndrome,' " Drew quoted. "We have all read it. Karen's too. What gave you the idea?"

"Uncle Llewellyn preaches in the local chapel when anyone turns up," said Gareth. "It's the same all over, dwindling congregations in all the churches. But go to the Moon and you come back converted, see? A well-known phenomenon it is. All I did was speculate why."

"Where did you do your research?" Drew asked him.

Gareth grinned.

"What research? I made the whole thing up, straight off the top of my head. It's a talent, see? The only thing I'm good at—telling stories. A born liar, according to

28

my mom. I always knew that one day it would come in useful. Never mind Canterbury Cathedral, here's where the big religious experience really happens. God is alive and well and living on the Moon. Never dreamed I'd actually come here though."

"That's quite astonishing," said Drew. "Your Lunacy Syndrome is uncannily accurate for a work of the imagination, and you are not at all what I expected. What do you think of Karen's essay?"

"That was something else," said Gareth. "Sheer magic, I thought, until I clapped eyes on her."

Drew nodded in understanding.

"She's even more surprising," he said.

Karen Angers was not at all what Gareth had imagined the writer of "Phoebe Unveiled" to be. He had imagined someone pale and quiet and poetic, a delicate, thoughtful girl he had been half in love with before he left Wales. But Karen was loudmouthed and gawky, an extrovert, and batty as an English cricket pitch. From the moment he had met her in the departure lounge at the Kennedy Space Center, everything about her seemed to grate on his nerves—her inane prattle, her constant gum chewing, her gee-whiz enthusiasm, her embarrassing familiarity. She had seemed to take possession of him, her touch on his arm demanding his attention. She called him Gary and was inescapable. And the ten tons of photographic equipment she had brought with her had made the trip to the Moon seem like a package tour. Now, looking at Drew Steadman with his keen gray eyes, white medic's coat, and dangling stethoscope, Gareth sensed a certain sympathy.

"I suppose you found nothing wrong with her?" he asked hopefully.

"I'm afraid not," said Drew.

"Did you try shining a light in her ear?"

"Meaning she doesn't hear too well?"

"Meaning you can probably see right through to the opposite wall. That girl's got a brain the size of a pea!"

Drew Steadman laughed.

"That's not nice, Gareth. Karen can't be that bad."

"She can't even get my name right!" Gareth said.

"It's only for one month," Drew said consolingly.

Four weeks on the Moon—that had been the prize offered in the international essay competition organized by the World Educational Council—one boy and one girl, under the age of eighteen, to be guests at the American base. And so they had arrived—Gareth Ewart Johns from Aberdare, Wales, and Karen Jane Angers from California, U.S.A.—on the regular freight shuttle at the end of an eighteen-hour flight.

Gareth's memory remained hazy . . . harsh light shining on the polished floor of the reception area . . . the click-flash of Karen's camera when he shook hands with Commander Bradbury . . . peculiar feelings of semiweightlessness and flight fatigue . . . roast-turkey dinner and champagne corks popping. His mind was a muddle of names and faces and voices and no person clear in it, except Karen—Karen with her shocking-pink travel suit, her photographic apparatus, and her overloud mouth, dominating the whole show. Gareth could have been in a hotel restaurant or a McDonald's. Karen had killed the Moon and destroyed whatever first impression he might have had.

And soon she would destroy the sunrise too, turning black to white as it swept across the dusty landscape. With her yak-yak, click-flash, hey-Gary drivel, he would gain nothing from it. She would turn it into a tourist spectacle, like Buckingham Palace on the King's birthday. Gareth needed to be alone, feel the Moon's almighty desolation, and catch the wonder when the sunrise happened.

"Is there anywhere I can go to be alone?" he asked.

"Evasion tactics?" asked Drew.

"If you like."

Drew frowned.

"I'm not sure I do like. Up here on the Moon we have to learn to get along, and you can hardly avoid Karen for twenty-eight days."

"How about half an hour, just to watch the sunrise?"

"The observatory should be empty at this time of day."

"Thanks," said Gareth. "How do I get there?"

Drew gave him directions.

"And don't stay too long," he warned. "Solitude can be dangerous on the Moon. Your Lunacy Syndrome has its dark side, Gareth, and human sanity is a fragile thing. Any funny effects I want to know about, right?"

"If I see any little green men, you mean?"

"I mean anything at all," said Drew.

5

The Moon was lonely. Gareth had sensed it even with Karen around. But now, having escaped her, he felt the impact. It was not the loneliness of Wales, mountains and bog and the curlews calling. Out on Pen-y-van was a kind of peace and grandeur. But here on the Moon was a loneliness that terrified, a monstrous isolation. Solitude was dangerous, Drew Steadman had said, and Gareth knew what he meant. No place on Earth could produce feelings such as these.

High on the catwalk of the domed observatory there was nothing to separate him from the stars. The immensity awed him—darkness and distance, a gold-black balance of time and space—infinite space, eternal time. Those stars had been there since before the forming of the world, before life evolved and apes became men. They would be there when the world ended and people ceased to be—fabulous shining suns, small as dust motes in the cosmic eye of God.

Gareth clung to the railing. Such thoughts brought everything down to size. All the achievements of the human race amounted to nothing, and individuality was swept away. His whole life would be less than a billionth of a second in the time scale of the stars. He was born and then gone, instantly snuffed out, a microscopic particle that momentarily flashed into existence before dying into oblivion. The realization of his own insignificance appalled him, and the terror grew. Mindless and insensate, the universe destroyed him, reduced him to a fragment of being, a tiny spark of life about to go out.

"God!" said Gareth. "You're supposed to be up here! Don't do this to me!"

Documented evidence suggested that few people returned to Earth unchanged by the lunar experience. Astronauts became evangelists, and hardened space technicians turned into religious gurus. Gareth had dubbed it the Lunacy Syndrome and tried to imagine it—some almighty mystical moment, an awareness of the sublime. But the Lunacy Syndrome had its dark side, Drew had said, and this was it—everything meaningless, including himself.

"Autosuggestion," said Gareth. "Damn you, Drew! And you can't stand it, can you? No," he said. "Best get out of here!"

He turned away, sensing the floor space far below him, seeing the great dome sweeping above his head, a shift in perspective.

Since the dawn of time men had looked up at the stars and called them heaven, generation after generation striving to reach them. Why? What was up there? Out there? Suddenly Gareth knew. It was a peculiar feeling, as if the fragment of being he had become detached itself from his body, swelled and soared, recognizing and knowing—the universe was not meaningless and empty, mere space and substance moving without purpose. It was deliberate and designed, charged with energy and power, a gold-black enormity in the mind of God of which all things were a part. And Gareth did not belong to the Earth. The stars were calling him toward them. The Moon tugging his heart. Terror changed to ecstasy. But then the lights snapped on and everything fled. He was back in his body, back in his own head.

Flaming Karen!

"Hey, Gary! Are you in here?"

Her voice echoed hollowly through the acoustic spaces, and the stars were gone among reflections of yellow light on the dome of transparent plastic. She put an end to Gareth's astral affinities, his intimations of immortality. Fifty feet below, in the well of the observatory, metallic glints showed on the mass of computers and radiographic equipment, and the sensation of height made him feel giddy. Instinctively he stepped backward, his weighted training shoes clattering on the metal gantry and betraying his presence. Karen looked up— a girl with long brown hair and a too-wide mouth standing in the doorway.

34

"Gary? Is that you?"

"Put the lights out!" he said.

"I'm coming to join you!" she shouted.

The observatory snapped back into darkness. Gareth heard the hum of machinery below and the rattle of her steps on the stairs, the clomp of her moon shoes along the catwalk. Then she was beside him, starshine in her eyes and the white gash of her smile, the inevitable camera hung around her neck.

"Hi," said Karen. "How's your headache?"

Gareth turned and leaned on the windowsill.

And she leaned beside him.

"Hi, Karen," she said. "I'm fine now, thank you for asking. And I'm sure glad you could join me up here. Gee, Gary, it's real sweet of you to say so. And you don't have to apologize—I only waited twenty minutes in the cafeteria for you to show!"

"How did you find me anyway?" Gareth asked.

"Drew told me where you were. He said the view is better from up here." She pressed her face against the glass. Her breath made mist on the plastic surface as she surveyed the barren landscape outside, the floodlit buildings, the black velvet sky, and the stars. "I don't see the Earth," she announced.

"It's below the horizon," Gareth informed her.

"Were you trying to avoid me?" she asked.

"Whatever gave you that idea?"

She touched his hand.

"I think it's real nice to have someone my own age," she said.

35

"The verb 'to have' implies ownership," Gareth said stiffly. "I'm not a consumer item."

"Okay," said Karen. "Then it's nice to *be with* someone my own age. It puts us together, I guess. All I want is for us to be friends, Gary. Instead of sneaking off, tell me what I'm doing wrong."

Gareth glanced at her.

Her chewing-gum breath was peppermint sweet.

And her touch went on.

"You really want me to tell you, girlie?"

"Well, I don't understand," she said. "I've tried my damnedest to be friendly with you, Gary. I know you English are apt to be reserved . . ."

"Right!" shouted Gareth. "Let's get a few things straight, shall we? You Gary me just once more and I'll jump on your bunions, girlie! The name's Gareth— G A R E T H! And I'm not English, I'm Welsh! I come from Wales, see? And I'm not used to being crowded. I like a bit of space between me and the next person. When I want to be touched up I'll let you know, but until then you keep your hands off me! You got all that, have you?"

Karen moved a respectable three paces away from him.

"Sure," she said. "I get it."

"Good," said Gareth. "Just stop chewing gum by my earhole and maybe we can be friends."

"You're not very nice, are you?"

"You did ask for it, girlie."

Karen fiddled with her light meter.

"Which direction does the sun come up?" she asked.

"Behind us," said Gareth.

"Drew says there are mountains nearby."

"The Lunar Apennines," said Gareth.

"I did some climbing at summer camp."

"Is that significant?"

"We could borrow some space suits and a buggy."

Gareth stared at her.

He could not believe she was being serious.

"It'll be fun," she said.

"You've got no more idea than the man in the Moon!"

"Woman," said Karen.

"Pardon?"

"She's feminine," said Karen. "Phoebe . . . Diana . . . the white Goddess. Every poet who's ever written has seen her as female. Haven't you read my essay?"

"Yes," said Gareth. "And it's got nothing to do with scientific fact. The Moon's not a flipping holiday camp!"

They might have argued, but then the sunrise happened. Karen stayed silent, and he did too, seeing the sun strike the distant mountains, stark white peaks floating in utter blackness, unsupported islands beyond the Mare Vaporum, Sea of Mists. They were sharp and spectacular, etched against the sky—Mount Bradley, Mount Huygens, Mount Conon, Mount Ampere—white as bleached bone.

"Snow tops!" breathed Karen. "Oh boy! That's really

something. Out of this world. Mind getting out of the way, Gary-eth? I want to get a shot."

"I don't know why you bother," Gareth said. "You can buy perfectly good postcards at the souvenir shop."

Click-flash, click-flash went Karen's camera.

"I didn't know they had a souvenir store here," she said.

"Every self-respecting moonbase has a souvenir shop, girlie. Moondust egg timers, moon-rock paperweights, ashtray craters, that kind of thing. You can hire skis too, if you haven't brought your own."

Karen looked at him suspiciously.

"Skis?" she said.

"They've got ski slopes on Mount Hadley," said Gareth. "Didn't you know? They run excursions twice a week."

Karen frowned and stared at the sun line creeping down the mountains. Soon a blast of daylight would hit the ocean floor, and already the plastic dome was darkening, reactolite blue, tingeing rocks and ridges with cerulean hue, filling clefts and valleys with indigo shadows. The harsh landscape was softened, its bleak beauty become a gentler thing.

"You're making fun of her," said Karen.

"Making fun of who?"

"Loneliness makes her cruel, you know."

"Who are you talking about?"

"The Goddess," said Karen. "The one the poets write about. She's ruthless and has no mercy. Don't laugh at her."

For some reason Gareth did not laugh. Poetic image or scientific fact, he caught the truth contained in Karen's words. The Moon *was* cruel. One careless moment and it would kill.

6

The base commander was waiting with Drew in the reception area, a burly middle-aged man in a navy-blue overall. Last night, in his United States Air Force uniform, Jefferson Bradbury had looked the part. Now, given a vacuum cleaner, he would pass for a moonbase cleaner, Gareth thought, everybody's favorite uncle, affectionately called J.B. But there was a hard glint in his eyes when he glanced at his watch, and an edge to his voice as he asked why they were late. Strict timekeeping was essential, he informed them, and Karen explained they had gone to the observatory to watch the sunrise. Breakfast smells drifted from the cafeteria, and Gareth's stomach felt hollow with hunger, but J.B. was taking them on a tour of inspection, so he fell into line.

"Can we go to the souvenir store?" Karen asked.

"What souvenir store?" J.B. asked.

"Gary says every moonbase has one."

One bushy eyebrow raised quizzically, and the steel gray eyes of the base commander fastened on Gareth. He saw humor in their depths and something else.

"The lad's a comedian," J.B. said to Drew.

"I'll make a note of it," Drew replied.

"There are no souvenir shops here, young lady," J.B. told Karen. "Maybe in fifty years' time . . ."

Doors to the main communications room opened and closed automatically, and the quiet corridor gave way to a barrage of noise. Low sunlight filtering through the reactolite windows turned Drew's red hair to a peculiar shade of puce. Faces looked gray and ill. Later, in the glass houses, plants bloomed with untrue colors in blue-green jungles of thick heat. Purple tomatoes fruited in Gareth's brain as they toured the swimming pool and recreation area, and went down in the elevator.

Like an iceberg city, most of the moonbase was below the surface—for insulation purposes, J.B. said. Normally Gareth would have been impressed. But the underground ways troubled him. The lights were too bright, and geometrical dimensions of walls and corridors and floor tiles played tricks with his eyes. He saw curving uprights and strange vanishing infinities. Distances telescoped, and, like Alice in Wonderland, Gareth felt himself either too big or too small. He even saw white rabbits breeding in the bio lab, and J.B.'s face was hatched with lines, a Tenniel illustration come to life, smile creased and heavy jowled. A thousand Karens, wearing caterpillar-green jump suits, reflected in the chrome fitments of the chemistry laboratory and blew pink bubbles of gum. Hunger, thought Gareth, was making him light-headed.

"What time's lunch?" he asked Drew.

They had hot dogs and doughnuts in an underground snack bar, but he still felt weird. Wherever they went—through all the kitchens and living quarters, computer rooms and research laboratories, workshops and power plants—Gareth was prey to the same bizarre impressions. Things assumed a nightmare quality, and his mind was woolly as a Welsh sheep's. He could hear his own voice asking questions, but the answers had no meaning. He could hear Karen yakking and failed to follow what she said. Absurdly Gareth wished that she would touch him, her hand on his arm confirming he was actually there. But he had drawn circles in the air around himself, and Karen touched Drew instead.

"Gee, this is fantastic!" she said.

It seemed to grow more fantastic with Gareth's every step. Walls keeled and floors sloped at idiotic angles—down or up, he could not tell which. His head floated and was unconnected with his legs. He swayed drunkenly, clutched a vending machine to save himself from falling, and its gargoyle mouth spewed coffee at his feet. Gareth stared at it, a pool of brown liquid shining stupidly in the light, contradicting all physical laws. And the floor dived downward like a playground chute.

"Are you all right, son?" J.B. asked him.

"You're supposed to put a cup underneath," said Karen.

"That was deliberate!" Gareth said wildly. "Waiting to get me, it was! I only touched the side of it! And who designed this place? Max flaming Ernst? Everywhere's wrong! I mean . . . look at it!"

"Look at what?" Drew asked quietly.

"Water flows downhill," said Gareth. "So why isn't it? And look at them angles! They're supposed to be ninety degrees! You ever been in the crazy house at Barry Island funfair? Makes you feel queer in the head, it does, but this place is worse. I can't stand it!"

J.B. pressed the intercom button.

And talked to the wall.

"Val? This is J.B. I'm in corridor D-seven. Have someone check this vending machine, will you? I also want a twelve-hour delayed countdown on that return shuttle. And get through to Medical. Tell them to send . . . ?"

"Fifty mils of B-thirty-six and a hypodermic," said Drew.

"You can't send Gary back to Earth!" shrilled Karen.

"He's severely disorientated," said Drew.

Lying on the bed in his own room, the funny effects stopped and reality stabilized. Horizontals and verticals remained true. His mind grew calm, soothed by the blue-gray daylight, the tranquilizing drug, and Drew's presence. He even accepted the color changes—puce hair, gray skin, forget-me-not walls. It was no worse than the orange streetlights in Aberdare.

"You won't really send me back to Earth, will you?"

"That's up to the base commander," said Drew.

43

"But there's nothing wrong with me now!" Gareth left the bed. "Look you—one leg, no hands—steady as a rock, see?"

He swayed wildly.

And Drew gripped his arm.

"I just need some practice," said Gareth.

"You need to lie down," said Drew. "I'll look in later."

Gareth lay still, listening to the soporific hum of the air-conditioning and refusing to sleep. He was annoyed with himself, annoyed with Karen. She stayed unaffected, her brain functions normal, but he was space drunk and incapable of controlling his body and about to be shipped out. He would never walk on the surface of the Moon beyond his window, or set his foot upon the Sea of Mists.

"Can't let that happen, can you?" Gareth asked himself. "No," he replied. "I got to practice. Mind over matter, that's what it is."

By the time Gareth reached the gymnasium, his coordination had improved. There were white lines marked on the floor for basketball games, and soon he could walk them all without falling over. Then he tried running. After that he did pushups, body bends, and balancing acts. And in the end he could stand on one leg even with his eyes closed. His confidence was restored. There was nothing wrong with him; now all he had to do was convince Drew and J.B.

At the sound of the meal buzzer Gareth headed for the cafeteria, but J.B. was not impressed to see him recovered. He was angry. Drew, apparently, had gone to check on him and found him missing, and the whole moonbase had been alerted. While Gareth had been holding a floor show in the empty gymnasium, they had been searching, fearing his space sickness might lead him to do something stupid, endangering his own life. Louder than the canteen clatter from the serving hatches were the base commander's whiplash words.

"I never thought," Gareth muttered.

"Then you'd better start thinking!" J.B. snapped. "Carelessness can cost lives up here! From now on you don't do anything or go anywhere without permission, right? And what's this garbage you've been telling Karen about ski runs on the Lunar Apennines?"

Gareth glared at her. She was seated in the window bay at the base commander's table, watching him anxiously, a hint of fear in her eyes. And outside on the launch pad the freight shuttle waited to take him home. Gareth was on probation in more ways than one.

"Permission to eat?" he asked Drew.

They dined on steak, served with sweet corn and reconstituted mashed potatoes, blue tinted and tasteless as straw. Gareth did not speak to Karen, nor did he speak to her afterward in the moonbase bar. He played darts with the freight-shuttle pilot instead, but all the while he could feel her watching him among the sounds of canned music and J.B.'s guffaws of laughter in the sapphire light. Later they went swimming. In the turquoise pool warm with sunlight, Gareth felt fully revived, and Drew's office in the morning no longer seemed a threat. But the enjoyment was gone out of

Karen, her chatter subdued, and going back to their rooms she trailed miserably behind him. Go to bed, Drew had told them, but Karen stood in his doorway. Flowers of indescribable colors wreathed her bathrobe, and water dripped from her hair.

"You got something on your mind?" Gareth asked her.

"Don't go," she said.

"You're the one who's going," Gareth said curtly. "It's ten to midnight, and I've got a medical checkup in the morning."

"Don't let them send you back to Earth!" said Karen. "I couldn't bear it here without you."

"Tough," said Gareth. "You should have thought of that before you opened your trap to J.B. Ski runs on the Moon! For crying out loud . . . you must have known I was joking!"

"Please Gary, you're the only one there is!"

"Gareth!" said Gareth. "So what's wrong with Drew?"

"He's twenty-eight, for Christ's sake! I need *you*!"

"I told you this morning . . ."

Karen shook her head.

Blue drops scattered, and there was fear in her eyes.

"You don't understand! It's not like that! You're the only reason I'm not scared out of my mind!"

"Scared?" said Gareth. "There's nothing to be scared of, girlie."

"Nothing," said Karen. "And that's what frightens me. I'd rather die than face that kind of emptiness. If you go back to Earth I'm coming too. I'm not staying here by myself."

Beyond her, in the corridor, the bright light darkened. Heavy shutters activated automatically and closed out the sunlight. Duplicating Earth time the moonbase simulated night. Daylight streaming through Gareth's window seemed incongruous now. Yet Karen waited, scared of it—the outside vacuum and the Moon's loneliness where no one was.

"I won't be going back to Earth," Gareth assured her. "I'll get up early in the morning and go for a workout. So you can go back to bed and stop worrying, girlie. The Moon's not seen the last of me. *Nos da, cariad.*"

"What?" said Karen.

"Good night, darling . . . in Welsh," said Gareth.

7

Bethkahn paced the ship's shining floor. Her red clothes
rustled in the silences, made scarlet flutterings in the
crystal pillars that arched and towered above her head.
A thousand images moved and danced as she passed
among clear glass tables and headed for the pool where
rainbow fish swam—biological specimens taken from
Athos Four, surviving as she had for ten thousand years.
Their fins made spectrums of the light passing through
them that flashed between dark reflections of lily leaves
and ferns. A jungle of plants glistened with damp drops,
roots feeding on a mulch of slime and fish bones and
their own decay. A small mechanized work unit with
robotic arms sprayed and cleaned and tended. Bethkahn
surprised it. Menial and voiceless it stared at her with
green unwinking eyes, then scuttled away. Work units
were programmed to be unobtrusive.

She sat on a padded bench seat among the rank scents of vegetation. She had come here to think, but the movements of the fish distracted her and she remembered how things used to be—curved windows open to a sweep of stars and the hall behind her alive with music and laughter. It had been a gathering place for off-duty crew—an intermingling of all the various departments, a kaleidoscope of uniformed colors, diaphanous, drifting—and robotic waiters served amber wine in tall glasses. Now the windows were smothered with dust, and the great room was silent, empty save for herself. But the memories stirred and ghosts teemed in her head—Rondahl and Mahna, Elveron planet finder, Dahn from Biology, and Keirharah who had taught Bethkahn to mind-sing.

Keirharah the enchantress, Rondahl had called her. On Athos Four, their second landfall, she had called its creatures to her—birds to her hands, horned sheep and wild cats walking beside her, day moths fluttering their wings in her hair. She had charmed the rainbow fish from sweet-water pools into Dahn's collecting jar, charmed away Bethkahn's initial shyness, and sung a softness into Rondahl's eyes. Keirharah would have mothered magic in her flesh-bred children, fostered a love of all that lived, a sense of worship and wonder. Perhaps she had taught them how to sing, her music in their language, in their minds—echoes of mists and rainbows, showers and shadows, of a landfall planet Bethkahn had never seen.

Words that were beautiful named the lunar seas. But

their Earth was not beautiful, the ship voice had said. Terrible things took place on it—motivations of greed and hatred and fear. Flesh had corrupted the souls of Rondahl's descendents, and the ship feared discovery. It was fear based on logic, it had said. Chances were it would be damaged beyond repair, Bethkahn captured and imprisoned, and home world become unreachable forever. Bethkahn thought of it longingly—Khio Three with its myriad milk-white towers, its blue-grass hills and gardens of flowers. The ship was the only hope she had of ever returning there, and she was bound to protect it, bound to do as it asked. She had to think of her future and disregard the past. But the ghosts remained—Keirharah singing in her memory . . . Mahna mind-hunting sand dragons on Chinnah Five . . . Dahn going white and golden among hanging vines. He was not forgettable—the flash of his smile and the searing blue of his eyes and the sunlight on his hair, honey colored . . .

"Go away!" she said.

"Bethkahn?" said the ship.

"You too!" she told it.

"I can't," it said.

Sometimes its logic made her angry—a computerized mind in a metal carapace hatching its plans. They could not wait any longer for Rondahl to return, the ship had decided. They had to escape from this moon as quickly as possible. Bethkahn must restore it to full functioning order—approach the American base, slip inside, and weld together the broken bits of stabilizer unit. It was all very simple and straightforward, except that somewhere, in order to avoid discovery, she would have to enter flesh, take possession of a human body. And that was not like catching a ride with Bahtoomi's deer, resting briefly within it, quiescent and experiencing, not interfering in its life or death. Bethkahn would be dealing with a being capable of conscious thought, an intelligence that might well become aware of her intrusion, that might refuse to share its body and decide to fight.

"I don't like it!" Bethkahn said definitely.

"Mistress?" said the ship.

"I've never done it before."

"It's standard procedure," said the ship.

"It's against the rules!" Bethkahn retorted. "We are forbidden to influence the physical, mental, or emotional functioning of any host creature we may enter. Even animals have a right to know and experience their own lives! That's why the Galactic Council was talking of outlawing evolutionary programs. They may even have done so, in which case you're asking me to commit an unlawful act. And if it isn't unlawful it's certainly unethical. It's unethical to force my way into another's body and override its will!"

The ship stayed silent, considering Bethkahn's objections. It was programmed humanely, to care for its crew and all life forms within it, to cater to their basic needs and harm nothing. It was for Bethkahn's sake it had planned their escape, but she talked of ethics, altruistic and often illogical, and questioned its morality. In the white light the great ship pondered and very carefully selected its words.

"I never suggested you use force, Bethkahn. I merely suggested you should share a body, hide within it, utilize its hands."

"And if it objects, what then?" Bethkahn inquired. "How else can I solicit assistance without taking possession? If the American beings are as dangerous as you say they are, they are hardly likely to cooperate, are they? Otherwise I could simply go to them and ask to borrow their welding equipment."

"There must be a way," the ship voice murmured.

"So tell me it," Bethkahn instructed.

"Keirharah would mind-sing."

"Not even Keirharah could mind-sing a whole moonbase," Bethkahn pointed out. "And we are not dealing with animals. These are intelligent beings, probably deaf to enchantments. And I am not Keirharah. I could maybe persuade a fish to feed from my hand but not a man to surrender his body and open his mind."

"It's your choice," the ship voice said stiffly. "You can either do as I suggest or not do as I suggest. But if you choose not to, I have already calculated the likely consequences."

Bethkahn bit her lip. Into human hands could fall a power undreamed of—a galactic spaceship and a girl who had come from the stars. Whether through fear, or desire, or curiosity, once discovered they would not be let go. And no harm would be done to the body she borrowed. She would simply be requisitioning it for a few hours of use, just a few hours to enter the moonbase, weld the stabilizer, and allow the ship to take off. However unwilling she or the Earth being might be, it was not much to ask. And maybe the ship's suspicions of human nature were unfounded? Maybe Bethkahn would find one who would agree to lend itself and co-exist?

"All right, I'll do it," she agreed.

"I bow to your decision, mistress."

"I shall need to know more about them."

"Details can be analyzed from my recordings," said the ship.

"And I may need to communicate with them."

"I have prepared hypnotapes of their language."

"I shall need a floor plan of their moonbase as well."

"That information will be stored in the cerebral memory banks of the host," the ship voice informed her. "You can extract . . ."

"Not if I'm denied access," Bethkahn interrupted. "If I take control of its mind then whatever he or she knows may be unavailable. I could end up inside what is virtually a walking corpse, in which case I shall need to know where I'm going. Why don't you tap their computer system?"

"I have already done so," the ship said loftily. "I took my knowledge of their language from their computers and almost betrayed my presence. They are alarm coded to deter infiltration by any outside agency. They assumed I was Russian, but I would hesitate to try again."

"You have to risk it," Bethkahn decided.

"If you insist," the ship voice muttered.

"And send down a scanner. We have to get closer. We have to observe these Earth beings. Once within flesh I need to know how to conduct myself. I need to know their routine, their relationships, their human habits."

"A scanner might be spotted," the ship voice objected.

"So might I," Bethkahn replied.

"I don't like it!" said the ship.

Bethkahn half smiled. Often in the ship's tones she had heard an echo of Rondahl, but now she heard an echo of herself. It was learning from her, adjusting its personality, subtly changing its role. She was a junior technician, and once it had been totally responsible for her. Now, if it was to fly again, it was dependent on her. And she sensed in its manner the true beginnings of a partnership.

8

In the shadows of the loading bay Gareth waited through the last few seconds of countdown. Inside his helmet, he could hear Karen chewing gum, the slow inhalation of Drew's breath, and the hiss of oxygen. Radiosensitive cells picked up every small sound. But the takeoff was silent. Silver in the sunlight, in a blast of dust and fire, the ship lifted slowly from the launch pad. Karen filmed it with her video camera, flames reflecting deep inside her head. And Drew was beside him, headless and burning, silver miniatures mirrored in his eyes. It might have been frightening, but Gareth focused his attention on the real thing—one Earthbound shuttle arching upward into the night-black sky, its flight path curving toward the stars where he belonged and being lost among them. Drew's voice sounded ultraloud across the suit's transmitter.

"There goes your escape route, Gareth!"

"Assuming I wanted to," Gareth said.

"That was fantastic!" said Karen. "Really fantastic! I never dreamed I'd get to film a spaceship taking off."

"If not for you I would have been on it," said Drew.

"Did you mind giving up six weeks of your leave?" Karen asked him.

"I volunteered," said Drew.

"Why?" Gareth asked suspiciously.

"Professional interest," Drew replied. "For those who come to the Moon there's usually a three-month training schedule, but you two have come here psychologically unprepared."

"You mean the first one to see a fairy sitting on a toadstool gets a prize?" Gareth asked. "Is that why you and Doctor Chalmers let me stay? To provide Karen with a bit of competition? A medical guinea pig, am I?"

"Not exactly," said Drew. "We let you stay because both Doctor Chalmers and I thought you could handle it, because you yourself wanted to stay, because Commander Bradbury agreed, and because you seem to be coming to terms with your symptoms."

"He's been up since five-thirty practicing," said Karen.

"Oh *has* he?" said Drew.

"Sure," said Karen. "He'd not have passed the physical exam otherwise. He was falling about all over the place, like someone drunk. We had to invent some co-ordination tests."

"You could park a moonbuggy in your gob!" Gareth said furiously.

"The ship's gone, so what does it matter?" Karen asked.

"It matters," said Drew, "because I don't like being hoodwinked! Because space sickness can be dangerous, and if anything happens to Gareth I shall be held responsible! I told you at the beginning—if you feel anything out of the ordinary I want to know! There's a Russian freighter due in at nightfall, so if you two are not very careful you're going to be on it!"

"See what you've flaming done!" said Gareth.

"How was I to know?" Karen muttered. "We're sorry, Drew."

"If Gareth so much as coughs you're to report it!" Drew said sternly.

"I will," Karen promised.

Gareth did not speak what he thought. It was all her fault—Karen with her big mouth yakking. She would be watching him now, waiting to squeal. And for the next thirteen days he would have to live with the uncertainty, knowing he was vulnerable, symptoms of space sickness waiting to take him over. He had only to give in to them, let go of his concentration. Grimly Gareth fixed his eyes on the stark sharp dividing line between shadow and light, followed it with his gaze. Visual distortions could be conquered by common sense. Whatever he saw, the angle between floors and walls was always ninety degrees, and the floors were always level. He refused to be fooled by any bizarre impressions. That was not a gigantic wheeled beetle squatting in the loading bay behind him, it was a common moon-buggy with black windshield eyes.

"Can we go for a ride?" asked Karen.

"Tomorrow," said Drew. "Today we walk."

Karen left her video camera in the air lock, and they headed out across the Sea of Mists. They had oxygen enough for three hours, heavy cylinders strapped to their backs made almost weightless under the Moon's low gravity. A clock dial on Gareth's wrist ticked away the minutes, its hand moving toward the red danger zone, which would trigger an alarm and give him twenty minutes to live. Such knowledge made life seem suddenly significant, but Drew said they would be back in the moonbase by then.

Brown-gray dust spread in all directions, featureless terrain except for the buildings behind them and the distant ridges toward which they were heading. Three elongated shadows moved blackly beside them. Balled yellow in the Moon's early morning, the sun hung low above the eastern horizon, detracting nothing from the inky spaces around it, but dimming the stars. Inside his suit Gareth could feel no heat from it. But in a few more hours, Drew said, they would be able to fry eggs on the rocks.

"So you can't grow daffodils on the Moon?" asked Karen.

"You can't grow anything," said Drew.

"And there are no pumpkin fields in Copernicus? Nor a pickle factory?"

"Who said there was?"

"Gary told me that by using bodily waste—"

"Gary?" said Gareth. "Who does she mean? Who's this Gary person she keeps talking about?"

"Karen," said Drew. "His name is *Gareth*. And you should know by now not to believe everything he says. Didn't you hear what J.B. told you yesterday? There's no climate on the Moon. There's no snow on the mountains, no rain, no wind, no air, nothing to support life."

"I was just making sure," said Karen.

"Pickle factory!" said Drew. "That's crazy!"

"Why does he tell such outrageous lies?" asked Karen.

"It's probably pathological," said Drew.

"I heard that!" said Gareth. "It's slander! And I come from a long line of Welsh bards!"

"In that case it's hereditary," said Drew.

The ridges were jagged against the sky. Gareth could see them from the window of his room. They seemed higher now, after half an hour of walking, but no closer. It was an effect of the foreshortened horizon, Drew said, which was something Karen failed to understand. Gareth could hear the mastication of her jaws, gum bubbles popping, her dumb questions as Drew tried to explain. An assault on his privacy it was, as if she was there inside his helmet, and Drew had forbidden him to switch off. But suit-to-suit transmission was limited to visual distances. If Gareth put the horizon between himself and them he would be out of range.

He quickened his pace, his shadow striding beside him, and the ridges ahead, mountains beyond and to the west of him. In full daylight the Lunar Apennines were not so spectacular—just humped hillocks or a series of molehills. High as the Swiss Alps, Drew said they were, but you needed to be among them to gain any impression of magnitude, for the curve of the Mare Vaporum lopped them off at the roots.

"If there's no weather on the Moon how come they called it the Sea of Mists?" asked Karen.

Once upon a time, said Drew, back in the sixteenth and seventeenth centuries, when the Moon was first charted and named, it was believed to have an atmosphere. Astronomers claimed to see mist or clouds in the Mare Vaporum, fog patches rolling out from the deep valleys of the Apennines. They even claimed to see live volcanoes.

"That one does look like a volcano," said Karen.

"Mount Conon," said Drew. "It's just a mountain with a crater on top of it, made by the impact of a meteor, just like all the others, or so we believe. It's possible we're wrong, of course. Our geological survey team has yet to go up there and check it. Could be Conon is a genuine volcano."

"So the old astronomers might have been right?" said Karen. "They might really have witnessed an eruption?"

"Hardly," said Drew. "Even if Conon *is* a volcano, it's been extinct for millions of years."

"But they must have seen something to make them believe," Karen persisted.

"Or else they believed first and then saw?" suggested Drew.

Gareth saw.

Something flashed high among the ridges . . . sunlight on glass . . . and flashed again, a blink of metallic brightness. "What's that then?" His voice, loud and intrusive, broke in on Drew and Karen's conversation. He turned to look for them—two small space-suited figures half a mile behind. They were no bigger than the plastic toys he had played with as a child. The impression terrified him—toy people and the vast loneliness around him, the moonbase gone beyond the curve of the horizon and something watching him. Gareth panicked, went running toward them, giant strides reducing the distance until they became life-size and human.

"Are you trying to take off?" Drew asked him.

"There's something up there!" Gareth said.

"Where?"

"Up there!" Gareth waved his hand toward the ridges. "Winking," he said. "A person with binoculars or a telescopic rifle. We're being watched!"

"I don't see anything," Drew said.

"Maybe it's someone from the Russian base?" Karen suggested.

"Or a bird-watcher looking for cuckoos?" said Drew.

"I'm being serious!" said Gareth. "We're being watched, I tell you!"

"Gareth!" Drew said warningly.

"I mean it," said Gareth.

"Okay," said Drew. "Try not to let it worry you. Keep a hold on yourself. I'll give you another shot of B-thirty-six as soon as we get back to base."

Gareth stared at him. He was Drew inside the dark glass helmet where the hills reflected, thinking Gareth was either clowning or sick. Based on an association of twenty-four hours, a history of pickle factories, white rabbits, and jackknifing walls, it was inconceivable that he could be balanced and rational and, for once, telling the truth. And, staring at the moonscape in Drew's helmet, he saw nothing moving or flashing among the high rocks in his face filled with boulders and dust . . . only a pint-sized silver figure that was Gareth's own self.

"Can I?" asked Drew.

9

The next morning they were scheduled to visit the Geological Research Station at Manilius, all day in a moonbuggy traveling there and back. But Karen refused to help load supplies. She complained of stomach cramps, and Drew believed her, so Gareth went out alone, testing his nerve as the air lock closed behind him. With a full three hours of oxygen he could have headed for the ridges behind the moonbase, but he did not trust himself to cope with the isolation. What had flashed up there among the high rocks would have to wait. His behavior was monitored, and a man by the name of Jake Kelly was expecting him to report to the loading bay. Gareth rounded the corner and crossed the concrete floor to where the moonbuggy waited. A space-suited figure humping boxes from the supply chute to the trailer paused to watch him approach.

"Are you Jake Kelly?" Gareth asked.

"You must be Taffy," said the man.

"Doctor Steadman told me to give you a hand."

Inside the trailer Gareth stacked the boxes that Jake unloaded from the chute. He was an immense man, tall and powerfully built and inclined to fat. His biceps bulged beneath the sleek fabric of his suit. He had been born in the Rockies and had worked as a lumberjack before coming to the Moon. Each box, which Gareth struggled to lift, Jake tossed toward him as if it contained nothing more than straw. Unstacked cartons piled up around him, and the thud of each one landing produced no sound, only an echo on the bed of the trailer that traveled upward through his feet.

"Will you slow down!" Gareth yelled.

The trailer creaked as Jake clambered on board.

"Put some backbone into it, Taffy."

Gareth heaved and sweated.

"What the hell's in these things? Lead, is it?"

"Pickled pumpkin," said Jake.

Gareth shot him a look. The shadows were deep inside the trailer, cutting down on the reflections. He could see Jake's face, bearded and grinning, the twinkle of his eyes behind dark glass. Now Gareth knew why the straight-faced scientists at the next table had smiled at him during breakfast, and why J.B. had said he was buying up shares in Heinz. Drew must have told the whole moonbase about the pumpkin fields of Copernicus.

"Daffodils and pickle factories," chuckled Jake.

"Damned good that. And the girl actually believed you? What else have you got lined up for us in the way of light entertainment?"

Gareth shook his head. "Nothing," he said. "I've got to watch myself, see? Any more funny business and I'll be shipped out on that Russian freighter that's due in at nightfall."

Jake laughed.

"Don't you believe it, Taffy. Our base commander knows what's good for us. You and the girl are a breath of fresh air as far as we're concerned, a genuine break in the monotony. He won't ship you out, and you'll soon find your moonlegs."

There was something reassuring about Jake Kelly. Hired for his brawn rather than his brains, he was blessed with a practical down-to-earth understanding of things. Space sickness was nothing to worry about, he said. He had suffered from it himself when he had first come to the Moon ten years ago. It wore off after a while. And it was nothing compared to some of the other psychological effects he had experienced. Driving alone over the Moon's barren surface Jake reckoned he had experienced most things.

"You drive alone?" Gareth asked him.

"Now and then," said Jake. "Now and then it happens I do. And all it takes is a mechanical breakdown and you're staring death in the face. That's when you start praying. That's when you find out whether or not Jesus loves you. Grown men weep out there, and scream. It's the silence, I reckon, the godawful loneliness of it. Sets

65

you thinking, it does. Then you begin brooding. That way you're heading for trouble. So you hang on to your pickle factory, Taffy. Laugh and the fear won't get you. We've all got our methods, and Drew Steadman knows it. Mine is to sing."

Jake's fine baritone voice filled Gareth's helmet with the Anvil Chorus as he stacked the boxes. Somehow it was hard to imagine the big man being afraid, yet he claimed to be—out there, where the sun smacked on the deserts of gray-brown dust, and the ridges rose, and nothing lived or moved, and the light flashed on a fragment of glass or metal, small and far away . . . once, twice . . . three times.

"Gotcha!"

Gareth straightened his back, fixed his eyes on a pinnacle of rock. Something shone among the shadows to the left of it.

"See that?" he asked Jake.

It took a while for Jake to locate the spot, and he could see nothing unusual. But unlike Drew he did not dismiss it as a figment of Gareth's imagination or a symptom of something wrong. It was probably a piece of broken satellite, he said. The Moon was littered with scrap metal—ancient orbiters that had crashed to the surface and broken up, defunct landing craft and unmanned survey machines, both American and Russian. It was a likely explanation and might have been acceptable, except that Gareth could have sworn he saw it move.

Click-flash.

"Smile please, Gary!"

Flaming Karen! Her taking photographs! And something reflecting her flash unit out on the ridges.

"Gareth!" he yelled. "My name's Gareth! Will you never learn?"

He leaped from the trailer, expecting the ground to strike but finding nothing until a few split seconds later, when he was already off balance. Click-flash. Karen snapped him as he crash landed on concrete and dust, and he did not see the answering flash from the ridges . . . he saw stars.

"I've come to see if we're ready to go," said Karen.

"*I* am," said Jake.

Gareth picked himself up. A sharp pain shot through his ankle, and his eyes watered. Space sickness was one thing, but Gareth felt like a walking accident. Jake half carried him back inside the moonbase. An X ray confirmed that his ankle was not broken, but it was badly sprained. Dr. Chalmers applied the strapping and advised him to keep his weight off it for the next few days. Wincing with every step and barely able to hobble, Gareth was hardly likely to do much else, and Drew considered leaving him behind. But Karen refused to go on the Manilius trip without him, so finally, with Jake's help, Gareth made it to the buggy, and the air lock doors sealed him inside. He watched the pressure gauge rising to normal.

"You can take off your helmets," said Drew.

Gareth switched off his oxygen, released the seals, and stowed his helmet in the space under the seat. The air was cool in the cab. He could hear the hum of the motor, and Karen's voice came suddenly loud as she too removed her helmet. She said the moonbuggy reminded her of an RV. It could seat eight and sleep four, Drew told her. There were emergency food and medical supplies, a portable-gas stove, and the toilet was in the closet at the back.

"If we get stranded," said Drew, "we can survive for days in one of these."

Jake flicked the radio switch.

"Echo to moonbase . . . time, eleven fifty-three. . . . We are signing out."

"Moonbase to Echo," replied a woman's voice. "You are an hour and twenty-three minutes behind schedule. We'll inform Manilius to expect a delayed arrival. Have a good run."

"We're not *likely* to get stranded, are we?" Karen asked worriedly.

"With Gareth on board anything's likely," said Drew.

Jake drove eastward into the morning. A crescent Earth hung blue through the side window, and Earth time made it almost noon, but the moonday had hardly begun. A low sun dazzled their eyes, and the landscape was dimmed by the dark glass windshield, barren deserts with nothing to see except tire tracks imprinted in the dust and an occasional route marker. It grew rougher later—the buggy lurching over stones where the ridges ended, and the trailer jolting behind. But mostly it was flat, visually boring, an unchanging horizon curving beneath a jet-black, starless sky. They talked some, ate canned-meat sandwiches and doughnuts, drank Coke from cans. Jake sang operatic arias, and the pain in Gareth's ankle eased to a throb. But outside nothing changed.

Manilius happened gradually after three hours of traveling—a line of low cliffs in the distance, rising higher and higher as they drew nearer, until finally the crater walls towered nine thousand feet above their heads. Jake stopped the buggy on the edge of its shadow for Karen to go outside and take photographs, but all Gareth could do was stare at it.

It was magnificent, awesome! Rising dark and sheer, a towering cliff over a mile in height . . . and Drew and Karen, absurdly small in their silver suits walking toward it. Her voice came across the buggy radio. It made the Grand Canyon look pretty stupid, she said. And Pen-y-van dwindled to a pimple in Gareth's head. He had traveled two hundred and fifty thousand miles to reach this place, but, sitting in the moonbuggy next to Jake, he was as far away as if he had stayed in Wales.

The Moon was unreachable and always would be. Men could no more experience it directly than goldfish could experience dry land. Not in a body of flesh and blood could Gareth walk barefoot through the dust, touch the hot rocks, and breathe in the airless spaces. He was trapped inside a mobile environment, inside a space suit, inside his skull.

But then he was not.

The moment that had happened high on the gantry of the observatory happened again. Some part of him came free. Detached from his body he knew no confines, no possibility of death. He knew he could go outside and live and he felt no pain in his ankle as he made for the door. Far far away, in another reality, he heard Jake whistling *The Pirates of Penzance*. Then, as his hand reached toward the button, something hit him. Hard fingers gripped and hauled him back and the voice of the big man from Wyoming blasted his mind.

"Are you out of your head, Taffy? What the hell are you trying to do? Kill both of us? The outer doors are supposed to be closed before you enter the air lock! And next time you want to go outside put your helmet on!"

10

Gareth might have killed himself on the trip to Manilius had Jake not taken action. He would never forget the shock of his own fear, Drew's alarm when he returned to the buggy, and Karen's face turned white with fright. What Jake had said was true—space sickness was nothing. Other psychological effects were far more dangerous. "Give way to unreality and you're dead!" said Drew. Gareth had to be alert at all times, awake to his own mind trying to deceive him, to the dreamlike feelings that now and then came stealing over him. Twice, on the return journey, Karen prodded him, and he thought she would never get his name right.

The next three days were spent at the moonbase, and Gareth was given a thorough medical check. He was even wired to the encephalograph machine, but his brain patterns proved normal, and his symptoms of space sickness were almost gone. Physically, Gareth was fit, except for the game ankle, which limited his ability to get around. But being at the moonbase was different from being in a buggy. There was room to move, solid ground under his feet, twice-daily video shows, pool tables and the swimming pool, and a computer library. There were people to talk to, things to do, and little chance to be bored. Outside, said Drew, it was boredom as much as anything that gave rise to peculiar mental states, and J.B. loaned him a pocket chess set.

"The moment you feel yourself slipping, concentrate on that," the base commander advised him. "Get some real difficult moves going. If you sharpen up your logic you're less likely to be taken in by anything that's illogical."

What had happened to Gareth was not so unusual, and everyone had their methods of dealing with the Moon's effects. Drew composed poetry. J.B. played chess, and Jake sang. But faced with the next trip Gareth felt nervous. It was only a hundred miles across the Sea of Mists to the outpost in Marco Polo, but almost immediately he began to feel strange. The moonbuggy bothered him—the soft hum of its motor, the vibrations, the feeling of confinement, and the monotony of the landscape outside. It was all too easy to let go of his concentration, sink into reverie, and cease to pay attention to the conversation around him. The chess set was meaningless. He wanted to get out.

Karen tapped him on the shoulder.

"Hey Gary! Are you still with us?"

Gareth rounded on her.

"My name's . . . oh forget it. Yes, I'm still with you. What do you want?"

"I was just checking," she said sweetly.

Her accuracy was uncanny, but after a while it became irritating. Again and again Gareth was forced to notice her—the peppermint scent of her chewing gum, her bilious yellow sun top, her jangling earrings, and her nonstop chatter. He did not want to know about the American way of life, her Mom's fashion boutique, her Pop's business enterprises, her kid brother's gerbils, the backyard swimming pool, and the beach house. For some reason the things Karen talked about made him angry. And just because he seemed unusually quiet did not mean there was something wrong with him.

"Will you quit poking me!" Gareth said savagely.

"So why don't you say something?" Karen asked.

"Because you never stop talking, that's why! And most of what you say is stupid! You want to try living in Aberdare for a few years. Never mind the private swimming pool and summer cottage—the only vacation we ever get is a cheap day excursion to Barry Island and a paddle in the sea! Uncle Llewellyn has lived all his life on Social Security payments, and Mom's been out of work for the last five years. All right for some, it is, but what about the rest of us?"

"I've heard things were bad in England," Drew murmured.

"Taffy's from Wales," Jake reminded him.

"And we've got it worse," said Gareth.

"You don't have to take it lying down," said Karen.

It was a discussion that lasted all the way to Marco Polo, ranging from Gareth's mother's fancy man and the upsurge of vandalism in Aberdare, to the Middle East war and the famine in Africa, and how Gareth did not have sufficient brains to gain a place in the university. What went on in the Welsh valleys was hardly Karen's fault, but it was one way of getting to know each other and plumbing the depths of each other's characters. They were four people putting the world to rights, and they paid no heed to the Moon. Gareth was unaware of the journey until they arrived.

Marco Polo was just another crater, and the outpost just another blue plastic bubble similar to the one in Manilius. It was home to three men and a woman—a metallurgist, a geologist, a cartographer—and Captain Slim Peters, who was a mountaineer from the U.S. Marines. They had corned-beef hash for lunch, and afterward Captain Peters escorted them up to the crater rim while Jake and the others unloaded supplies. Three space-suited figures climbed the narrow path, with Gareth limping behind. Inside his helmet voices of those below cheered him as he reached the top and were suddenly gone as he crossed the horizon and emerged onto the heights.

A scene of gaunt grandeur met his eyes. The rugged slopes of the Apennines were all around. The sun crept toward noon. Shadows were smaller, and the stark harsh contrast between darkness and light was even more intense. Valleys looked black and bottomless. Ridges, bone white, curved northward and southward like a monstrous spine. From the sheer edge Karen came walking toward him.

"Would you like to borrow my camera?" she asked.

"What for?" asked Gareth.

"Well, I never realized you couldn't afford to buy one and I've got others. So you can have this one. Keep it if you like."

"No thanks," Gareth said gruffly. "A memory is cheaper to run."

"I can let you have film," said Karen. "And you can get it developed in the moonbase darkroom."

"I think that's a very nice gesture," said Drew.

"But I wasn't looking for charity," Gareth objected.

"It's a gift," said Karen. "Happy birthday."

Her generosity embarrassed him. A camera was too much to give and too much for Gareth to accept. Finally, at her insistence, he agreed to borrow it. He took shots of Drew and Captain Peters with the mountains behind them, and Karen posed for him with a lump of moonrock in her hand. She said it had an odd shape and reminded her of something. It reminded Gareth of something too—the shape of a vertebra with a hole where the spinal column had once passed through. And Karen was gullible enough to believe.

"That's no stone!" Gareth said excitedly. "It's a fossil, see? A bit of fossilized backbone, look!"

"Hey Drew!" shouted Karen. "Look what I've found!"

"I heard," said Drew. "And it's just not possible."

75

"Well it sure looks like one!" shouted Karen.

"*Bovis lunaris*," said Gareth. "Part of the coccyx, I reckon."

Drew and Captain Peters took turns in studying it, their faces inscrutable inside their helmets, twin darknesses filled with stars. It was a stone that resembled a bone. Probably basalt, Captain Peters said. But Gareth was adamant. He could recognize a fossil when he saw one, and he had a talent for making the impossible sound plausible. It was proof, he said, of a prehistoric Moon where herds of *Bovii lunarii* grazed on the lichen that had once covered the rocks before the atmosphere seeped away into space. It hardly mattered whether Drew or Captain Peters believed him or not, they were willing to join in the search. Stones turned into carpi and metacarpi, and Karen found a fragment of rib. For her, *Bovis lunaris* became a reality, and its bones traveled back with them across the Mare Vaporum, an inexhaustible talking point.

"So what the hell *is Bovis lunaris*?" Jake asked.

"*Was*," said Karen. "They're extinct, you see."

"The literal translation is mooncalf," said Drew.

"Ah," said Jake. "I've heard of them."

"A close relation to *Assinus maximus*," said Drew.

"Herbivorous," said Gareth. "Monsters, they were. No natural enemies, see? The whole Moon got overrun. And once they'd eaten all the ground cover, stripped the place of oxygenating plants, they couldn't survive. It was quite a few million years ago—the equivalent of the early Jurassic."

"What I'd really like to find is a skull," Karen said wistfully. "Or a jawbone perhaps."

"Their last browsing ground was the mountains," said Gareth. "High rocky places where the dwindling vegetation still remained. We could try searching the ridges behind the moonbase."

"We could go there now," Karen said enthusiastically. "It's only a small detour and we've plenty of time before dinner. Can we, Drew?"

"Haven't you had enough for one day?" Drew asked.

He wanted a swim before dinner. He wanted an hour in which to relax. But Karen had made up her mind. He did not have to wait, she said. She and Gareth could *walk* back to the moonbase if Jake would drop them off. But not for one moment would Drew allow Gareth to go unaccompanied. He came with them, searching with Jake and Karen across the lower slopes of the ridge for the bones of a mythical creature he knew did not exist, while Gareth seized the opportunity. Fixing his eyes on the high pinnacle of rock, he headed upward, and not until Drew discovered a lump of fossilized dung did he notice Gareth was gone.

11

It was dark and soundproof inside the language booth, allowing no distractions. Bethkahn lay still. She had to empty her mind of all thought and become receptive, her only function to absorb. Preset, the hypnotape began to play, the voice of the alien computer reproducing its original learning program and teaching her to speak. No words to begin with, just the basic sounds of consonants and vowels and the corresponding symbols that appeared on the wall screen before her—the same sequence being repeated and repeated until Bethkahn had committed it to memory.

She pressed the PROGRAM ADVANCE switch and graduated to words, sounds, and syllables being strung together to form nouns and verbs, adjectives and adverbs. Pictures bestowed meanings—blue flower . . . laughing woman . . . run quickly. Slowly the hypnotape wound on. Sentences, which were infantile at first, grew in complexity as her understanding increased. Then the dull chant of the computer gave way to a human voice, and speech became music in her head. She no longer needed the vision screen. If she closed her eyes the words themselves invoked images, meanings that subtly altered with every change of emphasis, tones, and undertones sweet as Keirharah's song.

Through hours and days Bethkahn listened, and it seemed to her that some of them knew who they were—souls within flesh, aware of the immortal part of their being. From the man's voice reading she gleaned a thousand intimations, and intimations of other things too. Their human song could change within a single breath. Words told of blood and violence, of men who killed and were heralded as heroes, who committed murder and called it an act of love. She heard of mass slaughter made glorious in battle, hymns praising monstrous acts of cruelty and war. Both beautiful and terrible were the beings portrayed in the language Bethkahn learned, creatures of conflict whom she thought she would never understand.

How much of their speech and literature the starship had filched from the moonbase computers Bethkahn did not know, for she had no chance to reach the end of it. The ship's presence intruded. White light split the darkness, beat on her closed eyelids, flashed off and on, insistently, demanding her attention. The Earth beings fled from her head as she switched off the hypnotape and opened the language booth.

Shadowy and silent the great laboratory stretched away. Here were stored hypnotapes of every known galactic language and holograms of every planet they had visited—flora and fauna, climate and topography, culture if any. Once a dozen technicians had worked in this laboratory processing and programming the information gathered by the survey teams. Now it was dimly lit and eerie, long ago abandoned, and the ship voice echoed urgently among the filing stacks.

"You must come to the control room at once, mistress."

"Why?" said Bethkahn. "What's happened?"

"We are in trouble, I think."

Bethkahn moved swiftly. The lab shadows released her into a lighted corridor where her red clothes flickered like fire on the curved walls. There was a fear inside her worse than she had ever known. Something had happened that threatened the safety of her ship. Her ship . . . she had never thought of it in that way before. It had always belonged to Rondahl. But now, just recently, it had become a part of herself—a fifth limb, or a protective shell, an extension of her mind—and she would be helpless without it.

In Rondahl's chair Bethkahn took her place, brushed away the black strands of hair from her eyes. Waist long, it needed cutting, and her clothes were creased from a week in the language booth. Above her head the dark astrodome gleamed with stars, and around her the vision screens flickered into life.

"What's happened?" she repeated.

It was one more replay, seen through the eye of the scanner they had recently deployed. A telescopic lens showed her the blue domes of the American base, so close she felt she might almost touch them. Quite clearly in the loading bay she could see a water truck being filled, a gloved hand connecting the hose to the main tank. But suddenly the focus altered. A moonbuggy headed toward the ridge where the scanner was stationed, parked in the desert where the rocks began. Four space-suited figures disembarked and disappeared below the ledge. For several minutes the scanner waited motionless, then inched forward. Its lens angled downward, and Bethkahn gave a startled cry. A pair of blue human eyes were staring at her from behind the dark glass of a visor, and a moment later the scanner went blank.

"He found it?" she whispered.

"Yes," said the ship. "I did warn you of the risk."

"What shall we do?"

"You tell me," the ship said dismally. "They will take it to pieces, I expect. They will see it as alien, proof of our existence, and begin a search."

"I'll go to the moonbase and retrieve it," Bethkahn said.

"It's not in the moonbase," the ship voice muttered.

"Then where is it?"

"Right now," said the ship voice, "it is traveling in a southwesterly direction across the Sea of Mists. There is a time lag, you see, and I didn't want to disturb you."

Fifteen hours ago the ship had deactivated the scanner. Nothing functioned in it except the automatic tracking device, a small bleep of light on a grid map of the area. It had never entered the moonbase, the ship voice said. It had remained outside it, stationary aboard the moonbuggy.

"For fifteen hours?" Bethkahn said. "And you never informed me?"

"What good would it have done?" the ship voice asked. "I didn't know what to make of the situation. I can draw no conclusions and cannot advise you. I cannot fathom the workings of their alien minds. I don't understand what they're doing, Bethkahn. I'm afraid, and I don't understand!"

"Rerun the video sequence," Bethkahn said.

"How will that help?"

"There might be some clue."

The film flickered.

Blue eyes stared at her, just as before.

"Freeze it," she said.

Bethkahn studied his face among a host of reflections. He was young, she thought, younger than she was, an inexperienced youth. Maybe he had not realized the significance of what he had found? Maybe he had kept it to himself, not shared the knowledge of the scanner's existence? His blue eyes reminded her of Dahn and showed no hint of cruelty. Forgotten feelings fluttered inside her, butterfly wings of love and longing. It was not enough that the starship cared for her. She needed a person—a voice, a smile, another living being beside herself. And the boy had taken her scanner. She needed that too.

"There might still be time," she said.

"Time?" said the ship.

"The boy has our scanner, but I think he doesn't know what he has. He has shown no one and told no one, perhaps. They're not searching for us. They're out on a routine run, which means they will be returning. Track them. Tell me when you know where they're going. I can intercept them on their way back."

"Mistress!" the ship voice said in horror.

"Do you have a better idea?" Bethkahn asked it.

Protesting, the ship voice followed her along the labyrinth of corridors and into the wash unit. To act on impulse was a mistake, the ship voice said. Action needed to be planned. Silver drops showered from Bethkahn's hair. Warm air blowers dried her, and robotic work units sucked the moisture from the floor. Naked, in a hall of mirrors and wardrobes, she chose her clothes— gray misty trousers with a cowled overgown to hide her hair. Outside on the moon's surface she would be indistinguishable from the desert and the rocks. Blown dust would hide her movements from their eyes.

"And give us away!" snapped the ship.

"Until I enter the buggy," said Bethkahn. "Until I take him, enter the Earth boy's flesh. He can drive me back to the moonbase, and mend your stabilizer. One journey, one risk, and he may not fight me. I have to try it, don't you see?"

12

It was a silvery metal sphere the size of a soccer ball. At first Gareth had thought it was a bomb and was afraid to touch it. But who would plant a bomb on a moon ridge miles from anywhere? Common sense caused him to dismiss the theory, and he picked it up. There were several circles carved on its surface and five small holes bored into its underside. Held in his gloved hand it seemed weightless and hollow, a fragile mysterious thing. But he had no chance to examine it further. Drew blew his top.

It was understandable. Gareth had risked life and limb to climb the ridge and ignored all orders to come down. But he could not ignore the anger that simmered across the transmitter. Drew's message came loud and clear. He did not care what Gareth had found—a moon cuckoo's egg or a giant ball bearing from an alien spacecraft—if he was not back in the buggy within a quarter of an hour he would be answerable to the base commander, propelled back to Earth on the end of J.B.'s boot and never mind the Russian ship. With his fists full of bones from *Bovis lunaris*, and Karen beside him, Drew returned to the buggy to wait.

Having found the sphere there was no way Gareth would leave it behind, nor could he hurry. Slowly and carefully, mindful of the weakness in his ankle and its tendency to pain, he started to climb down, the sphere clutched to his chest. He was afraid it would drop, its eggshell-thin walls smash among the rocks. It took him thirty-five minutes to reach the buggy, and Jake drove away the moment he entered the air lock. Inner doors opened automatically when the air pressure rose to normal, and Drew was too mad to notice what Gareth smuggled inside—a silver sphere nestling in his upturned helmet and slyly transferred to the space under his seat.

The next morning, when they left for the satellite tracking station on Mount Serao, Gareth transferred it again—into a plastic bag saying WILLIAM'S GOOD FOOD STORES, ABERDARE LIMITED, along with his paisley pajamas and a spare pair of socks. And there it remained for the duration of the journey, like an itch that he could not scratch. He longed to take it out and look at it, but after all he had gone through to possess it he would not risk having it taken from him. Whatever the object was, it would have to wait until he returned to base.

Gareth had already decided it was some kind of robotic spying device. Russian perhaps? But he could not think why. High on the ridge it had been strategically placed to watch the moonbase, yet the Russians had satellites in orbit so why would they need a ground-based unit as well? Its purpose troubled him, nagged at the back of his mind, just as Karen nagged him to pay attention. She gave him no chance to ponder things out, and Drew was still angry. He banged Gareth's next fantasy squarely on the head. Those were *not* the infrastructures of gorgonzola mines, Drew said. They were the remains of Surveyors six and four, which had landed in the Sinus Medii over a hundred years ago. And not even Karen was prepared to believe the Moon was made of green cheese formed from the milk of the mooncalves' mummies.

"Better luck with the next one," Jake said.

"They wising up, or am I slipping?" Gareth asked.

"We're just getting to know you," Drew said darkly.

"Yes," agreed Karen. "And we're not *that* moronic!"

They stopped to take photographs and fragments of metal for souvenirs before driving on. Jake had taken the long route past Hyginus Rille and Chladni Crater, and now he turned north into the desert of the Sinus Aestuum. Earth time made it midevening when they drove up Serao's hairpin trail to the satellite base. The other moonbuggy, which had hauled the water tank, had arrived long before them and already unloaded. Gareth joined Jake in the trailer unstacking food supplies, and later Charlie Kunik, who was the driver of the Juliet buggy, played his guitar at an impromptu party.

Serao was a permanent base—three blue plastic domes on the mountain's summit, underground living quarters, and a staff of twenty. Solar panels gleamed silver in the sunlight of the Moon's high noon, and telescopic dishes were radio linked to those in the Mare Vaporum. On Earth it was long past midnight when Gareth went to bed—a sleeping bag on the backseat of the buggy and Jake on the front seat, snoring, while he lay awake. Sunlight filtering through the dark glass roof was impossibly bright, and the beer and barbecued beans he had had for supper gave him indigestion. He sweated in the heat of his sleeping bag and could smell the stench of his socks.

On the return journey the two moonbuggies traveled in convoy, heading south through the Sinus Aestuum. They would cut through the ridges, said Jake, and be back at the moonbase in time for the evening meal. A full Earth hung as a blue bead in a black-gloved sky. Sunlight faded it, said Drew. It was best seen at night, jeweled turquoise, shedding its light on the deserts of darkened dust. But still Karen insisted they stop to take photographs. Gareth yawned and waited. Deprived of sleep his eyelids felt heavy, and the air in the buggy was stifling and stale.

Jake nudged him.

"Either sleep or stay awake, Taffy. Do one or the other, but don't get caught between the two."

"Why not?" asked Gareth.

"Pink elephants," said Jake. "You're liable to start seeing things that aren't really there. Hypnogogic images, Drew calls it."

"Thanks," said Gareth. "I'll remember that."

He opened J.B.'s chess set and arranged the pieces, and Charlie Kunik driving the Juliet buggy had gone over the horizon before Drew and Karen returned to their seats and Echo was on the move again. Desert to the right of them and sun-baked ridges to the left. The lunar scenery was not conducive to alertness. It moved and swayed as the buggy moved and swayed, and was almost hypnotic. Gareth was hardly aware of the dozy sleepy feelings creeping over him until Karen poked him in the ribs.

"I was talking to you!" she drawled.

"Pawn," said Gareth, "to queen's bishop three."

"You don't fool me," said Karen. "You were miles away."

It was true. Gareth *was* miles away, being driven through a gaunt landscape of tumbled rocks and heading upward into the ridges. Half an hour of time had disappeared without trace. It was as if the moonbuggy and all its contents had suddenly been transported from the Sinus Aestuum to here. And the Earth beyond the window had changed its position. It shone in a blue halo around Jake's head, made him a bearded angel, the patron saint of the Moon's mobile grocery service ascending into heaven. Ahead the roadway ended in a sheer edge of sky. Gareth yelped and clutched the seat.

"For Christ's sake stop!" screamed Gareth. "We're going over the flaming edge! You've got to stop!"

"What's he talking about?" asked Karen in alarm.

"I don't want to die yet!" yelled Gareth.

A hand touched his shoulder, firm and strong.

"It's okay," said Drew. "Okay Gareth, just calm down. There's no edge, nowhere to fall. The trail goes up the ridge and down the other side. Look at it again . . . think about what you're seeing . . . concentrate your mind."

"Do you want me to stop?" asked Jake.

"Keep going," said Drew.

Quietly and calmly Drew kept talking, and back in his right mind Gareth realized he had seen an optical illusion. The Moon had fooled him with one more dangerous deception. He fixed his gaze determinedly upon the trail ahead, the high edge where the land ended and the sky began, waited as the buggy drove toward it and topped the rise. It was solid ground all the way to the moonbase—the trail winding down through a landscape of canyons and rock stacks and deep pools of shadow. Down and down and around the wall of a mesa. A few eddies of gray-brown sand swirled among the stones.

"It's a bit like Arizona," Karen said.

"The last stagecoach from Serao," said Jake.

"The wind's getting up," said Gareth.

"Is that the best you can do?" asked Drew. "Has your imagination finally failed you?"

"It's nothing to do with imagination," said Gareth.

"It's happening, see? Look you out there."

"God almighty!" cried Jake.

They rounded an outcrop of rock and he slammed on the brakes. Karen fell forward, cracked her head against the front seat, and the chess set fell to the floor, scattering its pieces. Saved by the safety harness, Gareth saw what Jake saw—the Juliet buggy crashed at the foot of a nearby cliff, its air lock door open, the driver slumped at the wheel. Without his helmet, Charlie Kunik was dead. And something moved at the mouth of the canyon, coming fast—a moonwind rising and a whirling tornado of dust.

Blood poured from a cut in Karen's forehead, but Jake did not wait for the living or the dead. Echo edged past the wreckage and sped as the moonwind moved toward them. Dust swirled past the windshield, obscuring Jake's vision, but Gareth saw to the heart of it. Someone was running—a shape without substance yet definitely there—a shadow girl, lithe as an Arabian dancer, her clothes gray and gauzy, her dark hair blown by the wind. Just for a moment Gareth glimpsed her, her face pale and beautiful and the dust whirling behind her eyes. Then she was gone, and the storm was gone, and Jake drove at full throttle down the empty trail.

"What the devil was that?" asked Drew.

"God only knows," Jake said shakily.

Gareth knew.

"Did you see her?" he asked. "Did you see what she was? Scheherazade, see-through as gauze. A flaming ghost!"

Karen dripped blood on her bilious yellow sun top.

"That's not damned well funny!" she screamed. "We might have been killed!"

"But I *saw* her," said Gareth.

And there at his feet, escaped from the confines of the carrier bag, rolled a strange silver sphere. Gareth stared at it in a moment of understanding. Hers, was it? The shadow girl who might have killed them? Looking for it, was she? Wanting it back? And had she killed Charlie Kunik instead? Slyly with his foot he kicked it back where it came from.

"I *did* see her," he said.

"Just shut up!" said Drew.

13

Bethkahn returned to the ship. Its hatches were buried, but the doors to the hangar bay remained open, blocked by a great dune of dust that had fallen inward. Bethkahn skidded down the slope. A bevy of robotic work units with vacuum-cleaner arms who had been set to clear it fled as she entered, retreating into the darkness. Their green eyes peered at her from behind the pillars, stupid mechanical things whose minds had only one purpose.

"You can get back to work!" Bethkahn said harshly.

Hearing her voice the ship switched on its lights. She saw the empty hangar bay stretching away, vast as a galactic conference hall. Her gray robes were mirrored in its shining floor, and from all around she could feel the starship watching her, its electronic sensors summing her up. She needed it, desperately. Maybe she even cared for it. But sometimes it was too much there, inescapable, witnessing everything, and she could not face the questions it was bound to ask. Tears shimmered in her eyes, and broken pieces of stabilizer rattled as she shed her backpack.

"You failed?" asked the ship voice.

"Isn't it obvious?"

"I told you not to go."

"All right! So you were right! There's no need to gloat!"

"What happened?" the ship voice asked her. "What went wrong?"

"I don't want to talk about it," Bethkahn replied.

"I've a right to know," the ship voice argued. "I'm the one who will be disemboweled if we should be discovered. I need to analyze the information—"

"I said I don't want to talk about it!" Bethkahn screamed. "Please!" she sobbed. "Please leave me alone!"

She wanted to run from it, hide from it, but there was nowhere to go. The ship was around her, everywhere, and she could not make such terrible confessions. She fled up the wide ramp to the basement corridor. Heavy metal doors barred the entrance to the ship's powerhouse, and a spiral stairway wound around the central column. Bethkahn took the steps two at a time, then paused on the first-floor landing. There was a circular lounge with alcove seats and picture windows showing a dozen different worlds—hologram landscapes that were deceptively real. She saw the golden cities of Cheoth One, whirru-birds flying above the purple plains of Korberon, and blue moonlight shining on the snow-capped mountains of Grath. And in between the corridors led away like spokes of a wheel.

It had been ten thousand years since last Bethkahn had visited these lower regions, the maze of passages and sleeping quarters that had once been assigned to the crew. But now she remembered her own room nearby, a second class cabin for junior staff with a door that closed to keep people out. Maybe the ship voice would not follow her there? Maybe it would respect her privacy and not intrude? Bethkahn sped down the corridor and shut herself inside.

The room was as she had left it—her sleep robe discarded among the pink crumpled covers of her couch. Music tapes were scattered on the floor where they had fallen, and a hologram image of her mother smiled from the wall niche among a garden of flowers. Kesha would have been informed of her disappearance, yet she smiled. She would smile forever under the sun of Khio Three, her blue dress blowing in the wind, among day moths that never died and everlasting flowers.

Her mother smiled as Bethkahn cried, wept for an ending she did not understand, the death of a man and her ignorance of his flesh. She wept for an Earth-born boy she had wanted and lost, and the mess she had made of things. She wept in despair, knowing what she had always suspected—that she and the ship would never escape from this moon. It was just a hope they had built up between them and tried to act out. Now it was over. A man had died, and Bethkahn could not try again.

Omnipotent within itself, the great ship watched her and wondered why she cried. It referred to all her past emotions, compared old causes, and saw no reason. It concluded this to be a new distress, a reaction to something that had happened outside and which the ship could not guess. Insufficient data, its computer banks said, and it did not know what to say to her or how to extract the information. It had to remain silent, waiting patiently, waiting until her tears subsided, and all it could hear was an occasional sob. It must be careful how it questioned her, and all it knew of compassion Bethkahn must hear in its voice.

"Mistress," it murmured. "I know I am only an unfeeling machine, and what you feel I cannot understand. I know I am not Mahna or Keirharah, but I am here and I do care. To the best of my ability I have always cared. I want to help you, Bethkahn, but I need you to tell me . . ."

Bethkahn raised her head. Strands of her dark disheveled hair clung to the tears on her face, and the silver shine of the ship's walls were all around her. It had a right to know, it had said. Its future depended as much on her as hers depended on it.

"He died," she said brokenly.

"The Earth boy?" it asked.

"The driver of the buggy," she said.

"You must tell me everything," said the ship.

Bethkahn stared unseeingly at the opposite wall.

"He died when I opened the door," she said dully. "Before I could even reach him. Instantaneously, without a cry, his flesh frozen and dead. And his soul stayed inside him, staring at me through his eyes, refusing to come free, refusing to forgive, silently screaming that I had murdered him. He didn't understand. He didn't know how to live without bones and blood. He just screamed and screamed, and I couldn't bear it, knowing I'd killed. You said the moonbuggies carried their own environment. But he was *dead*! And when the second buggy came around the corner I didn't know what to do. I was afraid I would destroy *him* too, the boy with blue eyes and those who were with him. I was afraid and held back and he *saw* me. He knows I exist! And if I open the doors of the moonbase I will kill them all! We're stuck here now, and there's no hope, not anymore."

The ship voice stayed silent, absorbing the things she had said and searching for an explanation. It had rifled the moonbase computers while Bethkahn had been away. It had taken floor plans, work schedules, blueprints, details of outposts and personnel files, anything it considered might contain useful information. Blueprints of a moonbuggy confirmed that each vehicle possessed an air-lock system. There should have been no escape of atmosphere when Bethkahn opened the outer door, not unless the inner door had foolishly been left open. Depressurization would kill instantly, but it was not her fault.

"It was an accident, Bethkahn," the ship voice declared. "It wasn't your fault. If the driver had followed the safety regulations he would not have died. You cannot blame yourself for the death of his flesh, mistress. You cannot give up hope."

"It is crime against life," Bethkahn said bleakly. "And I committed it."

The ship voice sighed.

She was not thinking logically, her mind clouded by emotion. And when dealing with emotion the ship was generally incompetent.

"Listen to me!" it said sternly. "That man's death was a mistake, and it was his mistake—not yours! If you come to the console room I can prove it. Now you must put it from your mind, Bethkahn, and next time we must allow for their carelessness."

"Next time?" Bethkahn said fearfully.

"There will have to be a next time," the ship said firmly. "And if the Earth boy saw you, it will have to be soon."

"I can't!" she cried. "I dare not risk it! I could not bear to murder him too!!"

There was no question of murder, the ship voice said. The moonbase was protected by a triple air-lock system. What had happened to the buggy driver could not happen again. It would be perfectly safe. They would work out her every move exactly, every small detail. They would study the work schedules, study the personnel files, choose the flesh.

"It must be a logical operation," said the ship.

"And that's easy for you," Bethkahn said sourly.

"One of us has to be," said the ship.

"I'm not leaving yet!"

"When you leave depends on what Gareth does," said the ship.

"Gareth?" said Bethkahn.

"His name," said the ship. "I have deduced it from the personnel files by a process of elimination—his age, weight, height, and the color of his eyes. Room A-forty-one. If he takes the scanner there we can afford to wait. But if he takes it to the laboratories you must leave immediately."

Bethkahn stared at the wall. His name was Gareth. Through a dark glass window his blue living eyes had stared into hers, and she could not forget. More than the dead man screaming murder, she remembered him.

"What else do you know of him?" she asked.

14

When Gareth claimed to have seen a girl near to the place where Charlie Kunik's buggy had crashed, no one believed him. It was a figment of his imagination, said Drew, a shadow perhaps, or a rock shape seen through the dust. The Moon had fooled him before, and not ten minutes previously he had suffered an optical illusion. If he used his common sense he would know it was impossible. There had been no girl out there, and there were no such things as ghosts—at least not on the Moon.

But despite what Drew said, Gareth was convinced he had seen her. Her pale face haunted him, delicate and beautiful, framed with drifts of dark hair. She was as real as the metal sphere he had smuggled into the moonbase in the plastic shopping bag. That night in his room he was able to examine it—two hemispheres fitted together, offering access to its innards if only he knew

99

how to open it. Later he would produce it in evidence, proof of the ghost girl's existence and as unearthly as she was. But first he needed a screwdriver, something fine and sharp to pry it apart. A nail file maybe? Karen was sure to have a nail file. But the corridor was dark and shuttered, the moonbase sleeping, and no line of light showed under Karen's door.

Gareth had to wait until morning, but with Drew at the breakfast table he had no chance to ask, and then J.B. came to join them. The base commander's eyes were hard as rivets, and coffee slopped from the cups when he banged down the file. He had just finished reading the preliminary reports, he said. Jake's account of what appeared to be an accident, and Drew's corroboration. It was all quite straightforward except for the ghost of Fatima dancing through veils of dust. "Hallucination—question mark," Drew had written. But J.B. suspected it was one of Gareth's stories, as ridiculous as pumpkin fields and pickle factories and, under the circumstances, in very poor taste.

"A man has died!" the base commander snapped. "And you'd better come clean, Sinbad! Is this one of your yarns?"

"No," said Gareth. "I *saw* her."

"Hell," said J.B.

"It's psychovisual," said Drew. "Remember the guy who thought he saw a mermaid in the Sea of Tranquility?"

Breakfast cereal crackled in Gareth's dish.

And the base commander sighed.

"Let's try looking at it rationally," he said.

Conversation was muted in the cafeteria around them, the atmosphere saddened by the news of Charlie Kunik's death. Gareth knew what the base commander was after, an admission, based on logic, that he had been seeing things. Across the table Karen watched him, a Band-Aid covering the cut on her left temple. She had been too busy bleeding to notice what had happened, and all Jake had seen was the dust. A storm of dust on a world without weather, whipped up by a moonwind that should not exist: that in itself was disturbing enough. Probably it had been caused by a moonquake that the seismographs had failed to register. Or possibly it was a new phenomenon, something never before encountered on the Moon's surface, inexplicable and dangerous. It was that possibility J.B. wished to rule out, along with Gareth's tale of a ghostly girl in gauzy Arabian costume.

"It was an illusion, son," J.B. said in exasperation. "You must *know* that?"

Gareth shook his head.

"I know what you want me to say. I'm not dumb, see? All right, she might not have been real. She might have been a mental projection or a dream image. But I can't swear to it, can I? I don't know if she was real or not. I only know I saw her."

Not for one moment did J.B. believe Gareth's account of things, but as base commander he could not take the risk. He had to allow for the possible existence of an alien life form. The whole moonbase was placed on standby, in a state of yellow alert. The fleet of buggies that were sent to recover the wreckage and Charlie Kunik's body were ordered to maintain constant radio contact, and the trip to Copernicus was temporarily postponed. Confined to base, Gareth and Karen spent the morning in the swimming pool with Drew giving them lessons in life-saving techniques. And J.B. at lunchtime said the dust storm had been confirmed by satellite recordings, but still no cause could be found. Through the blue window a single buggy was returning home, and Drew crammed the last of his sandwich into his mouth. He had to assist with the postmortem, he said, and for one afternoon Gareth and Karen would be left to their own devices.

"Try not to do anything stupid," he begged.

"Who? Me?" said Gareth.

"If there's anything you can't handle . . ." Drew said to Karen.

"I'll use the intercom," she promised.

"See you this evening," said Drew, and headed for the door.

"What's he mean, 'If there's anything you can't handle'?" asked Gareth.

"He means you," said Karen. "Who else would he be worried about? Funny things happen to you, or hadn't you noticed? Did she have a ruby in her navel?"

"You're dafter than I am," Gareth said.

"But not dumb enough to believe a story like that," said Karen.

"No?" Gareth looked at her. "Still got the bones of

Bovis lunaris, have you? Ever thought of getting them authenticated?"

Karen frowned at him—a girl with long brown hair damp from the swimming pool, her white flying suit made turquoise by the light. Seen in the high street of Aberdare, Gareth might have thought her attractive, but now ketchup dripped from her hamburger and suspicion showed in her eyes.

"What are you hinting at?" she asked.

"Nothing," Gareth said innocently. "But if you took them to the Geology Department you could have them carbon dated. Find out how old they are."

"I'll do that," Karen assured him. "And if they're not genuine . . ."

Gareth pushed back his chair.

"I'll leave you to it then."

"Aren't you coming with me?"

"They're your bones, girlie."

"Drew said we had to stay together! And I don't know the way!"

"I'll tell you the way," said Gareth.

Karen followed him back to his room. It smelled of sleep and staleness, and he had not made his bed. Dirty socks and last week's jeans and sweatshirt were strewn on the floor. More clothes spilled from his travel bag. A broken strut from Surveyor Four occupied the single chair, and his parka was slung over the back. A plastic shopping bag, saying WILLIAM'S GOOD FOOD STORES, ABERDARE LIMITED hung on the handle of the closet door, and two empty Coke cans rattled when he knocked against them. Gareth switched on the computer. Floor plans of the moonbase flickered on the screen, and Karen wrinkled her nose in disgust.

"Just look at your room!"

"The Photography Department is on Level B," said Gareth.

"It's worse than my kid brother's!"

"Geology is on Level C. Turn left at the elevator, and it's the second door."

"You haven't even unpacked!" said Karen.

"Level D is refuse and recycling," said Gareth.

"How can you live in a mess like this?" Karen grumbled.

"What's this?" said Gareth. "It's a blasted nuclear arsenal!"

"It's a blasted pigsty, you mean!"

"An underground silo!" Gareth said. "It's loaded, I tell you! I thought nuclear weapons in space were banned by international treaty?"

Karen unhooked the plastic shopping bag.

And threw it at his head.

"Put your dirty clothes in that," she told him. "We'll take them to the laundry rooms. No wonder Aberdare is a slum with you living in it!" She took the parka from his chair. "This is supposed to be hung up!" she said.

She had not been listening to Gareth, nor had he been listening to her, and before he could stop her Karen opened the closet door. A coat hanger rattled as Gareth crossed the room, slammed shut the door to the corridor, and stood with his back against it. And Karen could not fail to see the silvery metal sphere sitting on the shelf.

"What *is* it?" she asked.

"What's it look like?" he said. "It's a moonbuggy's egg."

"It's that giant ball-bearing thing!" said Karen. "You really did find it! Why didn't you tell us? Why didn't you show us? Drew mightn't have gotten so mad if you'd said you really had found it."

"I did say," Gareth reminded her. "And he didn't want to know. So now it's mine. And if you want to get out of this room intact you can keep your mouth shut about it, see?"

"Sure," said Karen. "If it means that much to you I won't say anything. Can I look at it?"

"Providing you swear not to tell."

"I swear."

Karen took it from the shelf, an orb shining with light, exquisitely fashioned and almost weightless in her hands. Gareth could see her face mirrored in its curve. She turned it carefully, noting the holes underneath it and the five curious circles carved in the smoothness of its surface. Its clear metal misted with the closeness of her breath.

"It's beautiful," she said. "I see why you want to keep it. But what is it?"

"Lend me your nail file," said Gareth, "and maybe we'll find out."

15

"Give! Damn you!"

All afternoon Gareth had been struggling to open the sphere, and Karen had got bored long ago and left him. Now, with it wedged between his knees, he once again applied the pressure, trying to lever the two halves apart. Nothing happened except that the nail file snapped and the sphere shot away from him, rolled hollowly across the floor. He was about to retrieve it when Karen returned from the Geology Department. There were tears in her eyes, fury in her voice, as she flung the bones of *Bovis lunaris* on his bed.

"Basalt!" she shrieked.

Gareth grinned at her.

"And basalt to you too, girlie."

"I'd like to kick your stupid teeth in!" Karen said bitterly.

"What have *I* done?"

"You made me look a complete idiot!"

"You shouldn't have believed . . ."

"I'll never speak to you again!"

"Have that in writing, can I?"

"And give me back my nail file!" Karen said.

It was broken in two. She threw the pieces back at him, told him to screw himself, and left, slamming the door. She did not speak to him at the dinner table and she spent the evening with Valerie Doyle from Communications, laughing and talking in the moonbase bar, while Drew stayed in his office writing the postmortem report. Gareth played darts with Jake and went to bed early, tried yet again to open the sphere and finally gave up. He needed something finer and sharper—a medical lancet, or a pocketknife perhaps.

The next morning Karen had still not forgiven him, and J.B. at breakfast was fuming about a falling-off of safety standards and people who were too damned lazy to lean over and press a button. Charlie Kunik had died from rapid decompression, Drew said, which would not have happened had he been driving with the inner door closed. It was assumed the impact of the crash had somehow caused the air lock to open, but what had caused the dust storm remained a mystery. They were running a full computer check in the hope of finding a clue.

Gareth was in the swimming pool when the base commander sent for him. He thought maybe they had found some proof of the ghost girl's existence and wanted to question him. But what they had found, J.B. said grimly, was a major security leak that was partly traceable to terminal A41 in Gareth's bedroom. Gareth tried to explain. He had searched through the floor plans in order to locate the Geology Department, but he knew nothing about any blueprints or work schedules or anyone's personal file. He was threatened with a full-scale investigation by the FBI, and life imprisonment for espionage. Alcatraz, J.B. said, was about to be reopened especially for him.

"But I never did it!" Gareth insisted. "I never touched them blueprints or anything else!"

He was blamed anyway, even by Drew.

In the lunchtime cafeteria Drew blasted him.

"I told you not to do anything stupid! I turn my back on you for one afternoon and straightaway you head for trouble!"

"All I did was look at the floor plans!" Gareth retorted.

"*And* the nuclear silo," Karen said slyly.

"That was an accident!"

"Don't give me that!" snapped Drew.

"I'm innocent, I tell you!"

"Innocent?" Drew said bitterly. "You only need to open your mouth and you're guilty of some gross misrepresentation of the truth! And I'm the one who is held responsible! I don't want to hear any more from you, Gareth! Not one word for the rest of the day! Or it won't be Alcatraz, it'll be instant lobotomy! Is that clear?"

Karen smirked and squirted mustard on her hot dog, and Gareth understood. For the rest of the day he had to pretend not to exist. It was not difficult. Karen would not speak to him. Drew would not speak to him. Jake was busy loading the supply trailer for the Copernicus run, and, with the moonbase on yellow alert, no one else had time. Alone among almost a thousand people Gareth watched Drew and Karen walk away. They were going to play pool. And he could either go and watch the afternoon video show or sit in the library and read a book, Drew had said. He was not even allowed in his own bedroom.

Gareth watched a film on flamingos, read the opening chapters of the *Zen Buddhist Handbook*, and practiced meditation—controlled breathing and his mind emptied of thought. He forgot his anger and resentment and entered a state of dark drifting calm. Images welled up from the depths of his subconscious . . . a transcendental being, beautiful and alluring, calling to him from the heart of dust. He floated toward her, leaving his body behind . . . imagined Drew finding it, sitting cross-legged in the moonbase library minus its occupant. It was one way of passing the time.

The dinner buzzer sounded, and back inside his body of flesh and blood Gareth found that nothing had changed. Drew and Karen and the base commander talked among themselves, and he was excluded from the conversation. Their laughter hurt, and the steak and french fries stuck in his throat, threatening to choke him. He did try. When he asked for the salt Karen passed it, but when he asked who had won the pool game he was ignored. It was unjust punishment! Every expression of his personality was being denied, and he might as well not be there. And if there were no more dust storms in the next twenty-four hours, J.B. told Karen, she could go to Copernicus.

"What about me?" Gareth asked loudly.

J.B.'s flint-gray eyes fixed on his face.

"You," said the base commander, "are a pain in the fundamental orifice, son. And where you're going I have yet to decide."

"Apologize, can I?" Gareth asked.

"Who to?" asked Drew.

"As far as I'm concerned you needn't bother!" Karen said sourly.

Gareth stood up.

"In that case I'll go to bed!"

"And keep your hands off that computer!" said J.B.

There was laughter behind him, but Gareth did not look back. He made his way to the table where Jake was sitting and asked if he had a pocketknife. Graham Sanderson, who was sitting next to Jake and worked in the Vehicle Maintenance Department, searched his navy-blue overalls. The knife had a naked woman on its hasp and several blades. It was a present from his girl friend in Pasadena, and Gareth promised to return it.

Late-afternoon sunlight was bright on the desert beyond the window of his room, the ridges sleepy with heat. He wanted to go out there, but the blue glass trapped him and the walls caged him in, and he did not like what had happened between himself and Karen, himself and Drew. He tidied his room as an act of atone-

110

ment, found J.B.'s chess set and Karen's camera. She had wanted to give it as a gift. A nice gesture, Drew had said, but Gareth had made her a laughingstock. Fragments of basalt rattled in the wastebasket, and the Geology Department snickered. She had really believed they were bones.

"How would you like it?" Gareth asked himself. "A nice girl, Karen. Generous. You should have gone for her, shouldn't you? At least she's real."

He sighed, smoothed the bedspread, and picked up the silver sphere. He was obsessed with a fantasy, a face in his head, dark haired and haunting him. Feelings, sharp as knives, shot through his guts when he thought of her. He had dreamed or imagined her, according to Drew, but the sphere was real enough. He could feel the grooves of circles beneath his fingertips, flush with the surface and varying in size. It belonged to her. He knew it belonged to her. But what *was* it? Gareth took the knife from his pocket and opened the smallest blade.

"Just one more go," he promised. "And if that doesn't work you're to hand it over, see?"

He pried at the center seam and failed to shift it. He pried at the circles one by one. Nothing happened. Then something did. A radio antenna shot upward, and the sphere came to life, sprouted arms or legs and jets of white light. Gareth yelped, dropped it in fright, but it did not fall. It floated on air, hovered and sank and slowly settled, its tripod legs finding the floor. And there it squatted, like a grotesque silver insect bent at the knees, its abdomen swiveling, its camera-lens eye panning the room until it fixed finally on him. Gareth cowered against the wall, expecting it to attack, send out a death ray aimed at his brain. His mouth was dry, and his heart hammered.

"Drew?" Gareth whispered. "J.B.? Karen? Somebody help me!"

The thing made no move. It simply watched him, positioned between him and the door. He reached blindly, feeling for something to throw at it, knock it off balance and make his escape. He found the camera and J.B.'s chess set. "Just stay where you are!" he breathed. Click-flash. One shot was all Gareth had time for before he hurled the chess set. It struck hard. Plastic split and pieces scattered as he dropped the camera and leaped for the door. He turned as he opened it, saw the robot thing swerve and recover, and slammed it inside. Gareth took one step and banged into Karen who was coming to look for him.

"Drew says if you want to join us—"

Gareth gripped her arm.

His face was colorless and she stared at him in alarm. "What's wrong?"

"It's got legs!" Gareth said wildly.

"What has?"

"In my room! It's got legs and an eye!"

"What are you talking about?"

"That giant ball bearing thing! It's a blasted robot!"

"Ha ha!" said Karen.

"Go take a look!"

112

Karen opened the door. There was nothing there—only a silver sphere among the chess pieces lying on the floor. It had withdrawn its appendages and become as it was before, lifeless and inert. Karen did not believe him, but Gareth believed. He was white and shaking and she could sense his fear. Give way to unreality and the Moon would kill. However infuriating Gareth was, Karen really did care for him. And at that particular moment he cared for her, needed her as he had never needed a person before—her warm flesh and her dumb conversation, her human sanity. A chewing-gum kiss brought them together.

"Tell me I'm not going mad," he said.

"You," Karen said softly, "are the maddest person I have ever met. Bananas Gary."

"Yes," said Gareth, "that's what I thought."

16

Bethkahn sat in the silver chair. The grief for the man's death was behind her now, her gray clothes changed for a midnight-blue tunic suit spangled with stars, anticipating nightfall. She had nothing to do except wait. Her flight path was charted. The navigational computer set to begin the countdown. And the scanner trace on the vision screen still remained stationary. Room A41, the ship voice had said, among the apartments assigned to temporary guests. With the next lunar dawn, Gareth would return to Earth, and it seemed to Bethkahn that he had no intention of handing the scanner to the moonbase authorities. As with the flower she had picked on Cheoth One and preserved in resin, he intended to keep it as a souvenir. Or maybe he kept it for another reason? Hiding the fact of her existence? Covering her traces?

Whatever his reasons, she had come to believe he would never give her away.

"We cannot trust any of them!" the ship voice had said. But staring at the bleep of white light Bethkahn smiled fondly. Gareth was giving her the time she needed—time to prepare herself, to be sure of her plan and eliminate the possibility of error. She needed to wait until nightfall and approach the moonbase directly under cover of darkness. Work schedules showed that the Earth beings kept only a minimum security watch during each sleep period, and the base plan layout showed there was a blind spot. If she approached from the ridges, due east beyond the furthermost dome, she would not be seen. The three main air locks faced south and north, but she would use the air lock in the loading bay— double doors for vehicle access to the Maintenance and Supplies departments, and single doors for personnel. A security checkpoint directly beyond noted the identity of all who passed out or in, but during the sleep period there was only one man on duty. That one man would become Bethkahn's flesh for the few hours she needed him—long enough to weld the starship's stabilizer, to make her way to Gareth's room and take back the scanner. She could abandon the body and leave before the moonbase awakened. No one would know she had been and gone. If the security guard had any memory he would think he had dreamed it, and only Gareth might guess.

"Seventy-two hours," Bethkahn said softly.

"Mistress?" said the ship.

"In seventy-two hours it will all be over. I shall be on my way back here and we can be gone from this moon."

"I wish it were sooner," the ship voice muttered.

"We agreed it's safer to wait until nightfall," Bethkahn replied. "Had Gareth been going to betray us he would have done it already."

With one last glance at the moonbase floor plans, the air lock blueprints, and the Earth beings' duty roster, Bethkahn cleared the vision screens and checked the internal scanners. Down in the hold the army of robotic work units were still clearing away the encroaching dust. It was nothing to worry about, the ship had assured her. If worse came to worst, it could blast itself free. Nothing could stop it taking off. But mixed with Bethkahn's joy was an underlying fear—that the ship was not space-worthy, that it was mechanically unsound and incapable of reaching Khio Three. If it should malfunction again she could be stranded on another empty world throughout another ten thousand years of loneliness. The thought filled her with dread. She needed someone—someone to talk with, to travel with her, to share.

"Have you checked your circuits?" Bethkahn asked loudly.

"All systems are functioning," said the ship.

"If you should break down on me . . ."

"I shall make it," the ship said confidently.

"Can you give me a guarantee?"

The ship stayed silent.

"Can you?" Bethkahn repeated.

"I am old," the ship voice finally admitted. "I am not the latest model, Bethkahn, and I should have had an overhaul a long time ago. I shall do my best, of course, but I cannot give you a guarantee."

Bethkahn understood. Something had changed between herself and the ship. Not long ago it would probably have lied to her or covered up the truth, but now it spoke openly as it would have done with Rondahl. Ten thousand years of immobility had done it no good, it said. It had been suffering from metal fatigue before it came here, and its innards were clogged with cosmic dust. Now, with the moondust and prolonged disuse, its condition had deteriorated. There was dust around its main vents, in its power housing and cable housing. There was a frayed wire in its hypodrive circuitry, and one of its conductor coils showed evidence of warping. It did not anticipate trouble during take-off, but it was worried about the vibrations during light-speed velocities.

"So how do you rate our chances?" Bethkahn asked.

"Fifty-fifty," said the ship.

"I'll replace the frayed wire," she told it. "And we can send in the microdroids to remove some of the dust. Maybe I can replace the conductor coil too."

"Not without assistance," the ship voice said.

Bethkahn bit her lip. It always came back to that. She needed someone . . . not just for her own sake but for the sake of the ship. Her psychokinetic powers were not sufficient to maneuver the conductor coil into place, hold it in position while she secured the connection. She needed another pair of hands, another mind. Bright stars on the astrodome blazed above her, and the scanner trace bleeped on its screen of white static. But the vision screen changed, even as she watched it, flashed into form and color. The stolen scanner had been suddenly reactivated, and her cry was involuntary. She was seeing into a room with blue-white walls, a view of distant ridges through a tinted glass window, and a blank computer screen. Then, as the lens panned slowly through one hundred and eighty degrees, she saw Gareth crouched in the corner—his blue eyes, his dark hair, his fear.

Bethkahn stared at him. Even in flesh his beauty made a pain in her, revealed the soul that swelled inside him, vital with life. She perceived the warmth of him, the depth of his being, his thoughtfulness, his humor. She wondered if he thought of her, after the man had died and their eyes met, if she for him was unforgettable. She watched him reach for the camera, saw the flash and saw him hurl the plastic box. Then, in one fluid movement, Gareth leaped and was gone, and Bethkahn was alone again, staring at a closed door, at white static.

The ship had deactivated the scanner, but the pain remained, cruel and terrible, a longing she could no longer ignore. She wanted Gareth, needed him, desperately, urgently. She needed him with her to have and to hold, enough to drag him from his body, his soul from his flesh—take him, make him come with her in a starship across the galaxy on a journey that might never end. She wanted to scream for the things she felt. She was afraid of her own love, her own desperation. Her fists clenched, and her fingernails bit into the palms of her hands. But the ship had a different fear.

"That's it!" said the ship. "There's an end to us! It was ignorance holding him back! Now that he knows what he has, he is bound to tell. We cannot wait for nightfall, Bethkahn. You must get to the moonbase as soon as possible—before they come looking. Do you hear me, mistress?"

Bethkahn raised her head.

She loved an Earth boy and could not go near him.

"I'll go," she said harshly. "I'll go there tomorrow, be there when their next sleep period begins. But I won't take back the scanner."

"You'll let our technology fall into alien hands? That's illegal, Bethkahn!"

"Not so illegal as murder," Bethkahn replied.

"Murder?" said the ship. "Who's talking about murder? I told you before—it was accidental death! And it won't happen again."

"Won't it?" Bethkahn said quietly. "We need him, don't we? We *need* the Earth boy. You need him to help replace your conductor coil, and I need him too. But more than that—I happen to love him."

The starship went into shock. She could feel it, dumbstruck in the white light around her. Somewhere in its data banks it would have the basic information about love, and eons of time with Rondahl must have taught it something. But trying to relate what it knew to Bethkahn and Gareth, and work out the implications, scrambled its computer circuits and left it temporarily stunned. Its light grew darker, and spluttering noises came from its voice box, and if Bethkahn had not felt like crying she might have laughed.

"Love?" squawked the ship. "You cannot love flesh!"

"I can love the spirit within it," she replied.

"His?" said the ship. "Predatory? Corrupted? His whole breed is bent on cruelty and destruction! He's not spiritually evolved, Bethkahn! He's not like you!"

"How do you know?" Bethkahn asked harshly. "How can you ever know? You're nothing more than a festering heap of scrap metal! But I know the rules, and you don't need to worry. I won't go near him, won't touch him, and you'll never learn how wrong you are! I'll just mend your stabilizer and leave!"

"And what about the scanner?" the ship voice asked stiffly.

"Gareth can keep it, do what he likes with it. They can all do as they like with it. I don't care! Why should I care? I'm not answerable for the actions of Rondahl's descendents—for a lousy planet in this far-flung arm of the galaxy! I'm just a junior technician . . ."

"And I could be dismissed from the service!" said the ship.

17

High on the walkway of the domed observatory Gareth and Karen stood together. A moonbuggy with its water trailer headed away across the desert—Jake, taking Charlie Kunik's place, making an emergency run to Marco Polo, where a broken valve had drained their supplies. Computers rattled down in the well of the floor space, and voices echoed as the men exchanged their duty shifts. Just for once Earth time and Lunar time co-incided. It was late evening, ten past ten by Gareth's wristwatch, and at any minute the Russian ship was due to fly past. Something worth watching, Drew had said. And taking Gareth's hand Karen had dragged him from the moonbase bar. Now with her arm linked through his, she snuggled close to him.

"This is nice," she said.

"Mmm," said Gareth.

"We could have been like this from the beginning instead of wasting a whole two weeks."

"Just don't get any ideas," Gareth warned her.

"I won't," she promised. "But I bet Drew suspects."

"Suspects what?" Gareth asked in alarm.

"I bet he suspects what's happened between us," said Karen. "We haven't fought for one whole day. But I haven't told him anything, if that's what you're worried about."

He relaxed again, seeing the buggy grow small in the distance and the sun, dim blue, through the reactolite glass hanging low above the Lunar Apennines. Tomorrow they would leave for Copernicus, but now the shadows were creeping toward him, and nightfall was only thirty-six hours away. And somewhere outside, on the Moon's barren surface, was an alien girl in whose reality only Gareth believed.

"She knows I have it," he murmured. "So what's she waiting for?"

"Who?" said Karen.

"That girl," said Gareth. "And that robot thing. It must contain some kind of tracking device. She wanted it back but she chose the wrong buggy, see? And when she opened the air lock Charlie Kunik died. Maybe that's why she didn't try it with us. But in the first place the sphere was on the moon ridge watching this base, so it must be something here she's after."

Karen stared at him.

"Are you being serious?"

"You ever known me to be anything else?"

"And you really believe . . . ? She's not *real*, Gary!"

"If she's not real then I'm nuts," Gareth said quietly. "But I know I'm not nuts so she *has* to be real. And there's nothing unreal about that ball-bearing thing, is there?"

"So what are you saying?" Karen asked.

"That somewhere outside is an alien life form," Gareth stated. "And you know her too, girlie. She's female, you said, and loneliness makes her cruel."

"I was talking about the *Moon*," said Karen. "Phoebe . . . the white Goddess . . . an abstract embodiment . . . the way men see her. Gee, Gary, you're not saying she's the one you saw? That's crazy! She's just a poetic myth!"

Gareth stared thoughtfully at the blue lunar landscape, the ink-black sky beyond the mountains where the sun dimmed the stars. It was here in the observatory that the Moon had really begun for him, thirteen days ago, in the first moments before morning. Since then it had changed everything, his whole way of thinking, his whole way of life. The Lunacy Syndrome—and he was caught up in it, no longer caring very much about his physical existence, caring more about his mind and soul, convinced he was more than simple flesh and blood. And the girl was a proof of it, an ephemeral being, discarnate and existing beyond death.

"Myths are rooted in fact," he said stubbornly. "And why, since the dawn of human thought, has the Moon been female? Race memory, is it? Maybe once upon a time we knew she was here. Maybe in the dim and distant past our ancestors visited here . . ."

"Space travel has only been around for a hundred years," Karen reminded him.

"How do you know?" Gareth asked her. "It might have been around for billions of years. It's conceit to think we're the only intelligent life forms in the universe! And the sons of God looked upon the daughters of the Earth and saw they were fair. Originally our ancestors might have come from the stars. Why else are we so obsessed with reaching them? And I'm not the first to put forward that particular theory. The whole of the was-God-an-astronaut brigade would back me up."

"All right," said Karen. "Suppose it's true. If the girl is real she must have lived here for thousands of years, so how has she survived?"

Gareth grinned.

"Gin," he said. "One hundred percent pure spirit. Like the Arabians used to keep in bottles and magic lamps."

"Oh very funny!" said Karen.

"Seriously," said Gareth. "I was reading about it yesterday in the *Zen Buddhist Handbook*. Everybody has an astral body. She's noncorporeal, see? A ghost, stranded here, wandering. My God, there's loneliness for you. She's probably desperate enough to try anything. And where's her ship?"

"Ship?" said Karen.

"She's bound to have a ship. How else could she have got here?"

"Flying carpet?" suggested Karen.

"You don't believe me, do you?"

Just then the Russian ship passed overhead. It was larger than the American transports—white with red fins and a hammer and sickle emblazoned on its side. It streaked low over the mountains, arched gracefully upward, and slowly sank, tail down in a blast of fire, toward the landing site in the Sinus Iridum. Nothing remained but the mountains, dark shapes edged with light, the cone of Mount Conon that the ancient astronomers had claimed to be a live volcano. They must have seen something to make them believe. Flames of a spacecraft landing perhaps? A belching of smoke or dust?

"Mare Vaporum," Gareth said softly. "Sea of Mists. But suppose it was dust? A dust storm witnessed from Earth that the ancient astronomers thought was cloud? A dust storm, Karen, blown by a moonwind. You saw it. I saw it. Even Drew saw it. And she's at the heart of it. Been here for centuries, she has. Bound to make a move soon, isn't she? Kill two birds with one stone, see? Take back her spying device and whatever else she's wanting. She can't trust me to keep quiet much longer."

"I think you should tell this to Drew," said Karen.

"Getting the wind up, are you?"

"If that girl comes here . . ."

"Not real, you said."

"But if she is . . . ?"

"Who's going to believe me? I've told Drew already. I've told J.B."

"You haven't told them everything!" Karen said urgently. "If you hand over that blasted ball-bearing thing they'd know you were telling the truth! They'd know it wasn't made anywhere on Earth! For crying out loud, Gary! You can't keep something like this to yourself! We could be in danger here! J.B. *has* to know! And if you won't tell him, I will!"

"Think he'll buy it coming from you?"

"Why shouldn't he?"

Gareth grinned and kissed her on the forehead.

"Remember *Bovis lunaris*?" he said.

"What?" Karen stared at him. "You mean it's another one of your little jokes?"

Gareth ducked as she swung at him, laughed and ran, his footsteps thudding along the metal passageway and down the stairs. Men in white coats watched with amusement or alarm as he charged between the computer banks, Karen screaming behind him as to how she would ram his blasted ball bearing down his neck, along with six jars of pickled pumpkin and a bunch of daffodils. Her rage, his laughter, drifted away along the corridor toward the guest bedrooms. They were young and lively—a breath of fresh air, most people said. But Karen did not think it funny. Her fists beat on the closed door as Gareth leaned against it, and her voice came muffled from the other side.

"I'm going to kill you!" Karen yelled. "You rotten lying swine!"

"Who says I was lying?" Gareth yelled back.

"What's that supposed to mean?"

126

"Work it out!"

"I'm going to tell Drew anyway!"

"You do that, girlie. He'll laugh his head off!"

"You'll pay for this, you Welsh oaf!"

"Nos da, cariad!"

"Don't 'darling' me!"

With one last kick at the door Karen went away, and, still leaning against it, Gareth smiled. He should not have told her, should not have involved her, but he had needed to test his theory, share the responsibility of knowing. She could either believe him or not believe him, tell or not tell. It was just one more of Gareth's fantastic stories. But whatever happened no one could say he had kept it to himself. Karen knew too—there was an alien girl intent on entering the moonbase. All Gareth had done was give her a few hours of time, another day or maybe two, bluff and double bluff until someone realized that he always had been telling the truth.

18

Gareth slept with her face in his mind, her dark hair and the shadows of her eyes. Then suddenly he awoke. Noise blasted his ears, a siren sounding the red alert. He sat bolt upright, thinking he was dreaming. It was twenty past two by his wristwatch, and he had forgotten to close the window blinds. The distant ridges were blue and still in the sunlight, but the siren went on and there were voices in the corridor and people running. Gareth leaped out of bed and pulled on his jeans. It was some kind of emergency, the start of a mass evacuation perhaps, and he did not have time to hunt for his sweatshirt. Naked to the waist Gareth opened the door, collided with Karen in her candy-pink dressing gown. He saw fear in her eyes, her face white as paste, and her voice screamed louder than the siren.

"Dust!" shrieked Karen. "She's coming, just like you said!"

"Who's coming?" Gareth asked in alarm.

"The girl!" shrilled Karen. "And Jake's out in the buggy. He'll be killed if she catches up with him! We'll all be killed!"

The corridor was dark. Blue light shone from their rooms and shone yellow from the elevator nearby when the doors opened. Security guards with laser guns came running past them, the base commander following behind, bawling instructions and buttoning his shirt.

"Never mind the oxygen loss! Just get that air lock open! Tell Kelly to drive straight in and we'll close it behind him! And turn off the siren!" With his shirt sleeves dangling J.B. turned his attention to Gareth and Karen. "You two can stay in your rooms!" he barked.

"What did I tell you?" Karen said wildly. "Jake's out there and she's after him!"

Gareth gripped her arm, propelled her across the corridor and into her room. She too had not closed the blinds, and the window faced across the open desert. He saw then why Karen was afraid—saw the moon-buggy heading home, and behind it, blotting out the horizon, was a great wall of dust. As a child Gareth had had nightmares about tidal waves, but now he was seeing one—a gigantic dust wave sweeping toward the moon-base, threatening to engulf Jake's buggy, engulf them all, as the siren wailed and Karen screamed beside him.

"Don't let it get me! I don't want to die! I want to

get out of here! Let go of my arm! Please, Gary! Let me go! Let me go! We're going to be killed!"

She screamed and struggled.

And he slapped her face.

"Don't talk crap!" he said harshly.

Karen backed away from him as the siren suddenly ceased, sat on the bed in the silence and touched her face. His finger marks showed an angry red, and he stared at her helplessly, then stared through the window at the buggy racing toward the loading bay and the desert rising behind it in the seconds before it struck. The sunlight dimmed. Dust blasted the window, hurled by a moonwind, savage and silent in one almighty demonstration of power. Gareth expected the moonbase to buckle and crack under the force of it, expected his own instantaneous death. But the storm passed over them and was gone as swiftly as it came. A few small eddies whirled across the landing pad and lay still. Human voices took over, and Karen sobbed softly in the aftermath of shock.

"The driver made it!" someone shouted.

"What the hell was it?" asked another.

And the intercom crackled.

"Maintain red alert. Top-level personnel report to their posts. We have an unidentified phenomenon. Repeat . . . we have an unidentified phenomenon."

"Inside or out?" Gareth said softly.

"It was true," wept Karen. "Everything you said was true! And we could have been killed!"

"It's not her intention to kill," said Gareth.

130

"How do you know?"

"I just do."

Karen took a handkerchief from her pocket and wiped her eyes.

"We've got to tell Drew," she said. "This time we've *got* to tell him."

"Tell me what?" Drew asked from the doorway.

"She's hysterical," Gareth said quickly.

"That's right!" Karen said angrily. "I'm hysterical! And you sure enjoyed slapping my face, didn't you?" She looked at Drew. "Do you know what Gareth's got in his room?" she asked. "A robotic spying device! He found it that day on the ridges. Someone's been watching this moonbase. He figures there's an alien spaceship nearby and that ghost girl he saw was real. She's the cause of the dust storm and now she's come *here*."

"See what I mean?" said Gareth. "Believe that and you'll believe anything."

"Out!" said Drew. "I'll deal with this."

Gareth returned to his room. He had maybe five minutes before Drew was convinced and came looking. Somehow or other he had to get rid of the sphere. Silver and shining he took it from the shelf in the wardrobe and stuffed it in the shopping bag, then put on his moonshoes and sweatshirt. Maybe he could dump it among the foam-rubber mattresses in the gymnasium? In the food supplies or linen supplies? Or bury it in the glass houses among the tomato plants? Why he should take such a risk he hardly knew. It was just something he had to do . . . for the sake of the girl.

Cautiously Gareth opened the bedroom door. The corridor was dim-lit and empty, the panic over and no one about. He headed away toward the recreation area, but he had not taken more than a dozen steps when the intercom crackled. "Doctor Steadman . . . your assistance is required at number three air lock," a woman's voice said. "Will Doctor Steadman please report to number three air lock immediately." Karen's door opened in response and there was nowhere Gareth could hide.

"Where are you off to?" Drew asked.

"The lavatory," said Gareth. "What's going on in number three air lock?"

"Search me," said Drew. "In the morning I want a word with you. Officially. In my office. Nine-thirty sharp."

"Karen tell you everything, did she?"

"She told me enough," said Drew. "And Karen's impressionable enough without you filling her head with rubbish, especially at a time like this! We've got enough to contend with as it is, and we don't need aliens!"

"I won't tell her no more," Gareth said solemnly.

He opened the bathroom door. Harsh light shone on Drew's red hair, showed the mock severity on his face, and the shopping bag rustled as Gareth sidled past him. A fast hand caught his arm.

"I'll just have a look at it," said Drew.

"A look at what?" asked Gareth.

"Whatever you have in the bag that's causing all the fuss."

It might have been the end of everything, but away in the distance, toward the Vehicle Maintenance Department, someone screamed. It was a terrible inhuman sound that seemed to go on and on—a man screaming in agony or anguish, or the maddened howling of an animal in pain. Broken metal smashed against the walls, and someone came running, a pale shape at the dark end of the corridor heading toward them, footsteps pounding. Seeing them Dr. Chalmers skidded to a halt. His white coat was ripped to tatters. There was blood on his face and he was breathing heavily.

"Steadman . . . thank God it's you!"

"What's happened?" Drew asked in alarm.

"The buggy driver," Dr. Chalmers gasped. "Something's radically wrong with him. He's fighting like a madman. Homicidal. A danger to himself and everyone else. A full-blown psychosis, it looks like. A voice in his head, someone taking over his body. He's broken one guy's wrist. The base commander got a fist in the face, and no one can get near him. I'll go get help and the hypodermic. You get down there. He's in the main storeroom."

Dr. Chalmers went running on toward Medical.

And Drew turned to Gareth.

"Do what you have to, and go back to your room," he said quietly.

"Was it Jake?" Gareth asked sickly. "Was it Jake he was talking about?"

"Just do as I ask," said Drew. "And don't say anything to Karen. I'll talk to you in the morning."

He was gone then, walking away. Darkness dissolved him and Gareth entered the bathroom. Light shone on white-tiled walls, and thoughts whirled in his head. Human sanity was a fragile thing, and Jake, who had known the Moon as no one else, who had sung in its solitude, had gone insane. Something terrible had happened to the big man from Wyoming. What had he seen in the heart of the dust storm? What had pursued him across the deserts of the Sea of Mists? The alien girl? The one Gareth was protecting? Some kind of devil wanting to possess him, was she? Taking over Jake's body? Her voice heard in his head?

Mirrors on the wall above the sinks reflected Gareth's face—pasty pale from lack of fresh air, his dark curls tousled from sleep. It was his fault, what had happened to Jake. He had known all along the girl was real, and he should have reported her. He should have shown Drew the sphere and made him believe. Loneliness made her cruel, Karen had said. She had killed Charlie Kunik and it might have been deliberate. Now she had taken Jake's mind, and that might be deliberate too.

"Know what you've got to do, don't you?" Gareth asked himself. "Yes," he said grimly. "You've been had for a sucker, boy, and never mind her looks. First thing in the morning, one alien ball bearing for the base commander, definitely and without fail."

He nodded and entered the stall.

And a few minutes later he left with the shopping bag.

19

When Gareth left the bathroom a man's voice shouted.

"Hey! You!"

He turned in alarm. Two security guards were coming toward him, black shapes in the semidarkness with a shine of light on their hard hats. A white gauntleted hand pointed a laser gun in his direction, and a flashlight shone on his face, dipped as he was recognized.

"Gareth!"

He eyed them warily.

"Going to arrest me, are you? Unlawful urination during off-peak hours?"

"This is the smart aleck who broke into our computer banks," one guard told the other. "Been late-night shopping, son?"

"Not exactly," said Gareth. "It's something I picked up, see? A robotic spying device from an alien space-

135

ship. Going to give it to the base commander, I was. Available, is he?"

The first security guard gripped Gareth's arm.

"Okay, funny guy, let's have you back in your room. With a full-scale search going on we've no time for games."

"This is important!" Gareth protested.

"You're darned right," said the guard. He frog-marched Gareth down the corridor. "Room A-forty-one. In you go, fruit cake. And stay out of the way."

Gareth paused with his hand on the door handle. Way up ahead there was daylight and voices in the main reception area, and back along the corridor the other guard was shining his flashlight in all the unoccupied rooms. In the gloom and silence Gareth could sense it— the night full of disturbance, the atmosphere bristling with unease. They were looking for someone, and Gareth knew who. She was alien and dangerous, and she was inside the moonbase, and sooner or later she would come looking for him.

Room A41—the luminous number was painted on Gareth's door. He had only to go inside and lock it, but his skin prickled as he opened it, and he almost cried out. The room was in darkness, blackness so absolute it made a wall against his eyes. Someone had lowered the window blind in his absence, and when he felt for the light switch the electricity failed to work. His heart missed a beat. Someone or something was inside his room, hidden and waiting in the unrelieved dark. He could actually feel a presence. Fear paralyzed his muscles and dried his throat. And the security guard watched him, the beam of the flashlight sweeping toward him. He had one split second to make up his mind.

"Gareth?" someone whispered.

Flaming Karen!

Gareth entered the room, closed the door, and leaned against it. She had scared him stupid, but now he wanted to laugh at his own fear. He waited for the security guards to clear the immediate area, listened to the pitch-black humming of the air-conditioning and his own breathing, their footsteps moving away along the corridor.

"What the hell are you playing at?" he said.

Magically the strip light in the ceiling began to brighten, a dim illumination slowly gathering strength. Gareth saw the room whitening around him, the outline of the bed and someone standing beside it. He caught his breath. She was not Karen. She was insubstantial as a mirage in the desert, yet he could see her exact in every detail—the blue shimmer of her clothes, the pallor of her face, amber eyes and drifts of dark hair. He could see the computer screen through her midriff and the shadows of the alcove behind her. Nervously biting her lower lip the alien girl regarded him, waiting as Gareth stared at her through the first few seconds of shock.

"You!" he said.

"Don't give me away," she begged.

"How did you find me?"

"Room A-forty-one—my ship took the information

137

from your computer. I didn't mean to come here but I didn't know what else to do, who else to turn to. Help me, Gareth. Please help me."

She was not like Karen. She had his name right and her voice was quiet, strangely accented, yet perfectly distinct. Her pale hands were held toward him in a gesture of appeal. Gareth clenched his fists. Only five minutes ago he had decided to hate her, but her amber eyes held him, beautiful and deep, and there were feelings inside him he did not know how to cope with. But he was not about to trust her. Her ship thieved knowledge, and he got the blame. Charlie Kunik had died from her actions, and Jake had been driven insane. Hesitantly the ghost girl moved toward him.

"Don't come any closer!" Gareth said harshly.

"My name's Bethkahn," she said.

"Stay away from me!"

"I won't harm you," she said.

"So what happened to Jake?"

"Who's Jake?"

"The buggy driver you came in with. No harm, you say, but what did you do to him? Raving, isn't he? And you're responsible for that."

Her expression crumpled. He saw a look of anguish in her eyes that was replaced by weariness. Her whole body sagged in defeat as she slumped on the chair and ran her fingers through her waist-long hair. She had so much power, but whatever had happened between her and Jake had left her beaten. She stared at the floor, shuddered as she remembered, and he wanted to pity her. But his voice was ruthless and he needed to know.

"What did you *do* to him?" Gareth repeated.

"Nothing," she said brokenly. "I did nothing. He was too strong for me, and I couldn't control him. He wanted to kill me, tried to destroy me . . . destroy himself and everyone else. All that rage, and hatred, and horror . . . those terrible feelings. I couldn't stay in him, couldn't bear it. I tried to talk to him, but he wouldn't listen, wouldn't understand. I only needed his body for a few hours of time—the use of his flesh, the use of his hands. I wouldn't have harmed him, no more than I would harm you. It's against our laws to damage life. I left him in the storeroom. They said he was mad, but it wasn't my fault. It wasn't!"

She raised her amber eyes to look at Gareth.

Her eyes watered in the light.

"What about the other buggy driver?" he asked. "Charlie Kunik, the one who died?"

"I never meant to kill him," she said. "I never intended . . . But I'll live with it now—his death on my conscience—my ignorance, my mistake. Those feelings just now—I'll live with them too, and the damage I've done to the mind of a man. I wish the ship had never woken me. I wish I'd slept forever, never come here, never learned of you."

"So how can I help you?" Gareth asked.

"I wish there was another way . . ."

"Just tell me what you want."

"I dare not risk another mind . . ."

Gareth stared at her.

Suddenly he sensed Jake's horror.

"You want to borrow *my* body? Come inside and take possession? Hell's flaming bells! You really expect me to . . . No way, girlie! Help's one thing, but not that!"

"I'm not asking for that!" Bethkahn said vehemently. "Not from you, Gareth! Just mend my stabilizer, that's all. And give me back my scanner."

Gareth smiled in relief and held it toward her, a shopping bag saying WILLIAM'S GOOD FOOD STORES, ABERDARE LIMITED, then looked where she pointed. There was a bag on his bed, not transparent as she was, but bulky and substantial and made of some toughened gray material. Scrap metal clattered when he opened it and tipped out the contents. It was some kind of rotor blade with two of its arms sheared off. It needed welding, she said. Without it her ship could not take off, and she had been stranded on the Moon for ten thousand years.

"Alone?" he asked. "For ten thousand years!"

"Except for the ship," she replied.

"What happened?"

It was a strange tale Bethkahn told. She was a junior technician aboard an interstellar spaceship. It was her first voyage, she said, and something had gone wrong with the ship. They had landed here, on this moon, to make repairs. It was just a broken stabilizer, a routine replacement. The rest of the crew had left her to it, taken the survey craft and gone to explore the nearby Earth. They had never returned, she said. Their survey craft were destroyed in a volcanic eruption when the island continent sank beneath the sea.

"Atlantis?" gasped Gareth.

"I don't know," she said. "I only know it happened, that I was stranded here. And the laser packs were empty and there were no spare stabilizers on board. I thought I would be here forever, alone forever. I couldn't stand the loneliness of that. So my ship let me use the cryogenic chamber. Sleep was the only way I could forget. And then it woke me, told me you were here, and finally I came."

"I'm glad about that," Gareth said softly.

"I didn't want to come," Bethkahn confessed. "But I had no choice. One day your kind would have found me, held me captive for the knowledge I possess, and taken my ship apart."

"You make us sound like ogres!"

"Not you," Bethkahn said quickly.

"I'm no different," said Gareth.

She stared at him.

Her amber eyes softened and his insides lurched.

"Aren't you?" she murmured. "I think you must be. Why haven't you betrayed me, Gareth? Why did you keep my scanner and give it to no one else? Why, after the buggy driver died and you saw me, didn't you tell? And why are you sitting here now, talking to me, instead of raising the alarm? Will they help me, Gareth? The ones who are searching? Will they mend my stabilizer and let me go free? Will they?"

"No," he said.

"Then why are you?"

20

The storeroom was dark, a concrete cavern full of stacked boxes, with narrow windows set high in the apex of the roof, where dim blue sunlight filtered through. Somewhere in here was Bethkahn's escape route—a service air lock that led directly to the loading bay outside. She stared about her, trying to get her bearings, her amber eyes raking the shadows between mountains of supplies. The air was pungent with unfamiliar scents of dried fruit and spices, and the cold storage units made a soft humming of sound. Gareth's breath was white mist beside her.

"Over there," he said softly.

Bethkahn followed him. A forklift was parked by the wall, and beside it a ramp dived down into the darkness of the air lock. She regarded it nervously, reluctant to commit herself and reluctant to leave the boy from Earth whom she would never see again. She wondered if he felt as she did, but just for the moment Gareth paid her no heed. Instead he studied the control panel. Dual control buttons opened and closed the hatch, and a square of green light showed when he flicked the switch.

"Do you know how to operate it?" Bethkahn asked anxiously.

"No," he said. "But I'm about to learn."

"Maybe there's another way out?" she suggested.

"The main air locks will all be guarded."

"The corridor wasn't."

"That was my good judgment and your good luck," said Gareth. He slung the shopping bag containing the scanner down the well of the service chute. "Now you," he said.

"It's so dark," she said nervously.

Gareth looked at her.

Shrewd blue eyes fixed on her face.

"Don't want to go, do you, girlie?"

She shook her head and her lower lip trembled. Maybe he saw and understood why, for he suddenly reached out his hand. He was trying to touch her—a lock of her hair, the curve of her neck, the blue soft fabric of her tunic top and the nebulous warmth of her being beneath it. He touched and his hand passed through her, and she was not tangible, not to him, no more than light or air. He sighed, knowing it impossible, sharing her sadness in a moment of finality.

"It's been nice," he said thickly. "Nice meeting you, girlie. You've taught me a lot. Same underneath, we

143

are, but you've got to get out of here. Your ship told you right. If anyone should find you, they won't let you go free. You've got to go while the going is good, see, and leave it to me."

Bethkahn wanted to cling to him.

But she made herself smile.

And her voice stayed calm.

"Good-bye Gareth," she said.

It was hard to leave him, hard to turn away from him, but Bethkahn had promised the ship. She entered the black gap of the air lock and slid down the ramp. The hatch door closed behind her, shutting her inside a claustrophobic space as dark as a tomb. There was no chink of light, no movement, no sound but the rustle of the plastic bag, until the mechanism wheezed into life. An unseen door opened before her and sent her catapulting through. This time she was in a depressurization chamber. She could hear the suction pumps working, feel the vacuum around her, and the last hatch opened onto a blaze of natural light. An emerald blindness temporarily deprived her of vision as she slid down the supply chute to fall among dust and shadows on the concrete floor of the loading bay.

For a few moments Bethkahn lay still, stunned by the emptiness and silence that flesh could not survive. Noises heard inside the moonbase echoed in her head. She felt giddy from the change of pressure. Then she picked herself up, picked up the bag with the scanner, ran for the nearest buggy, and crouched between its wheels, its bulk hiding her from anyone who might approach. She could see beyond the shadow line the sunlight of the open desert and the distant ridges stark against the blackness of the sky. Just a few meters of concrete between herself and freedom. But she had to wait awhile before she made her final escape. She had to allow Gareth sufficient time to return to his room. For her sake, as well as his own, he could not be caught in the corridor when the alarm siren sounded the next red alert.

Slow minutes slipped by, time imagined in her mind like the tick of his wristwatch or the beat of his heart. In thirty-six hours she would leave this moon, but all she could feel was a kind of grief. She had lived through the loss of the whole ship's crew, but it seemed as nothing compared to the loss of Gareth. Almost, she thought, she would be leaving behind her own soul, and knowing him made the loneliness a thousand times harder to bear.

"Stop it!" she whispered. "Stop it, Bethkahn!"

She pushed the thought of him from her, preparing to run. It was mind over matter, and she needed to concentrate. Dust particles shifted, swirled across the concrete, and were drawn toward her. The moonwind rose, and the dust grew thicker, whirling around her, veiling the sunlight beyond. She was the eye of the hurricane, the vortex of the storm that moved as she moved, a towering tornado bursting from the loading bay and sweeping away toward the ridges. She knew what she was to those who watched from behind the blue glass windows of the moonbase—a thing of terror they would never understand.

With the dust gone behind her Bethkahn climbed the ridge, searching for shelter among the high shadows of the rocks. The sun was poised above the rim of the mountain crater where the starship was. Mount Conon, Gareth had called it, named after a barbarian hero in a comic-strip book. The ship would not be too happy knowing she had told of its whereabouts, but right now Bethkahn did not want to think about the ship. She looked back at the moonbase, a sprawl of buildings on the distant horizon, glowing blue and golden in the last long hours before sunset. She tried to pick out Gareth's room—somewhere between the domed observatory and the arch of the loading bay—wondering if he too was standing at the window looking out for her.

And in the sky beyond the moonbase was the Earth from where he had come, turquoise blue and three parts full. A madhouse, Gareth had said, all right for those who had money but not much joy for the rest. It had been beautiful once, he had said, but now it was spoiled by idiot men, and he did not rate its future prospects very high. Almost Bethkahn had offered to show him the gardens of Khio, the golden cities of Cheoth and the rose-pink worlds that revolved around Bahtoomi's star. It would have been easy to tempt him, but she had held her tongue.

"Tell me where you come from?" he had asked.

"It's just an ordinary planet," she had replied.

"In another dimension?"

"Only in distance."

"You mean I could go there, just as I am?"

"It's nine thousand light-years," she said.

He understood. He would be dead before he reached it, his flesh turned to dust. Bethkahn did not tell him he would also be alive, his spirit traveling beside her, enduring through time. She could have persuaded him that his flesh did not mean very much, but one man's soul had screamed to her of murder, and she was afraid that those who were born into bodies could not live free of them. Emotionally Gareth was bound to his flesh, and Bethkahn gave him no hint of hope or possibility. Underneath they were the same, he had said, but she would not take him from the people he knew, from the man named Drew and the girl named Karen, and the planet of his birth.

Bethkahn's eyes watered in the Moon's sunset light. She moved to sit in the lee of a boulder, sighed and settled, the bag at her feet. WILLIAM'S GOOD FOOD STORES, ABERDARE LIMITED, it said, in green and red lettering. It was all she had to remind her of Gareth— a shopping bag and the memory of a meeting that should never have happened.

It should never have happened, but it had, and Bethkahn could not forget. Ridiculous . . . serious . . . he could change in a moment, and she had met no one else like him. Impossible to reach to the depths of him, distinguish the difference between truth and lies. He had told her of Earth, and she had listened, appalled to hear

of the evolution for which her kind was responsible, the
extent of injustice and cruelty. Yet that same evolutionary program had produced Gareth—his intelligence, his awareness, his quality of caring. No, he was
not forgettable—his smile, his laughter, the glorious
strangeness of it after all these centuries of time.

She sighed and tipped out the scanner. By this time
in the Earth's tomorrow she would owe Gareth a debt
of gratitude that she could never repay. Leave it to
him, he had said, and she knew she could trust him.
One mended stabilizer would be sent down the supply
chute for collection during the next sleep period, and
all she had to do was wait . . . wait, as the starship was
waiting—an unfeeling machine, its tireless computers
fearing what had happened to her, wondering and worrying and programmed to care. Fear was logical, it had
said. Bethkahn activated the scanner, waited for the
lens eye to find her, and started to signal.

"I shall be twenty-four hours late in returning. . . ."

21

Sleep was his alibi. Gareth ignored the wail of the siren, raised voices, and footsteps running. He ignored Karen when she came to his room. "Can I come in?" she asked plaintively. His eyes stayed shut and she went away, and a few minutes later the siren sound ceased. The next thing he knew was Karen shouting him awake, the scarlet glare of her blouse seen through the squint of his eyes and her gold necklace glinting in the light.

"Who let *you* in here?" Gareth said sourly.

"It's twenty to nine," she told him.

"And I'm tired."

"Tired?" scoffed Karen. "What have you got to be tired about? Most of us have been up all night, but you slept right through it. You never even heard!"

"Heard what?" growled Gareth.

"At twenty to five this morning there was another

red alert," Karen informed him. "I came here needing company, scared out of my skull, and you never even woke up! Four hours I've been sitting in my room waiting for morning, and who cares? I've never been so lonely in all my life. And all you've done is lie in bed and snore!"

"Can I help it if I'm a heavy sleeper?" Gareth muttered.

"You must have cloth ears!" Karen concluded. "And if you want breakfast you can't lie there any longer. Gee, Gary, please get up. I've got no one to talk to and I'm scared all on my own. Please get up."

"You want to try it for ten thousand years, girlie."

"Try what?"

"Nothing," said Gareth. "Just get out of my room and let me dress."

When Gareth entered the cafeteria Karen was sitting alone at the table in the window bay, crumbling a cracker and sipping orange juice, staring bleakly around the almost empty room. Canned music played in the background, but the room contained a mood and a silence. A few morning faces were grim and haggard from lack of sleep, and no one smiled. He collected ham and eggs from the serving hatch and went to join her.

"Where is everyone?"

Karen shrugged.

"I guess they're busy. That's what I was telling you. No one bothers with us anymore, not even Drew."

"We're on our own then?"

"It sure seems like it."

150

Gareth almost smiled. The less people bothered about him the better. It suited him fine—no Drew, no base commander, no organized itinerary. Everyone was preoccupied with last night's happenings, and he could do as he liked. He could go to the Vehicle Maintenance Department, use the welding equipment with no one peering over his shoulder and asking what he was doing, or why. He only needed to be rid of Karen.

"We were supposed to be leaving for Copernicus this morning," Karen said gloomily.

"You can forget about that," Gareth told her.

"So what shall we do instead?"

Gareth looked at her, swallowed a mouthful of ham.

"You mean what will *you* do? I've got something on for the rest of the morning."

Karen stared at him.

Blue feelings flickered in her eyes.

"Are you saying you don't want me around?"

"I never meant it like that," Gareth said quickly.

"So how *did* you mean it?"

"I've just got a few things to do, that's all."

"Like what?"

"Socks," said Gareth. "I've got to wash some socks, for one thing."

"That should take you at least ten minutes," Karen said sarcastically.

"Plus half an hour to write some notes, an hour looking for the pawn I've lost from J.B.'s chess set, and two hours explaining to Drew about that load of bullshit you sold him last night. And why should I be accountable to you for my time? Not bound to stay together, are we? And have you never wanted to be by yourself? There's quietness out on Pen-y-van, girlie, and I need it, see? I told you that right at the beginning."

But the fact remained—Gareth wanted to be rid of her and she knew it. The hurt actually showed in her face. But there was nothing he could do about it, no way he could explain. The disk of the sun hung low above the rim of Mount Conon, where a crippled starship lay, and all he had was this one day. Tonight Bethkahn would return to the moonbase, and her need was greater than Karen's. She would be trapped here forever if Gareth did not help her.

"I'm sorry, girlie, but that's how it is."

"Screw you!" Karen said viciously.

"Meet you for lunch, I will."

"Don't put yourself out!"

"Ellen!" J.B. shouted. "Bring me a coffee!"

Karen turned her head at the sound of the base commander's voice, smiled as he came toward them. He was smartly dressed in his Air Force uniform, but last night's happenings had taken a toll. Dark circles ringed his eyes. He needed a shave, and a purple bruise showed on one cheek, where Jake had hit him. He heaved a sigh as he sat beside them, waited for the serving woman to bring him coffee, then turned his attention to Karen.

"Well, young lady, how are you this morning?"

"I never slept a wink," said Karen.

"That makes two of us," J.B. said.

"What happened to your face?"

"I . . . er . . . walked into a door."

J.B. stirred sugar into his coffee.

And glanced at Gareth.

"Are you all right, son?"

"As well as can be expected under the circumstances," Gareth replied.

J.B. nodded.

"Yes," he said. "And under the circumstances I think it best if the two of you return to Earth. There's an investigative team arriving this evening from the Russian Base, and Bronski has agreed to a delayed takeoff of the Soviet ship. We're waiting for a U.S. Government clearance for it to land at Kennedy, plus confirmation from the Kremlin, but you leave on the Russian hopper for the Sinus Iridum tomorrow morning. They've had no disturbances over there, and as we don't know the dangers involved I'd rather you were both gone from here. I'm sorry to cut short your stay. It's been nice having you. . . ."

"I'd rather leave anyway," Karen said.

"It's the only thing to do," said J.B. "Under the circumstances. We'll contact your parents, and Drew will be traveling with you. Okay with you, son?"

"No," said Gareth.

"Well, I can't stop to discuss it now," said J.B. "I'll see you this evening, but I won't be changing my mind."

The base commander swilled his coffee and left. Gareth stared at the egg yolk congealing on his plate. It was all settled. Come tomorrow he would be going home, back to Earth, to the gray hills of Wales, Mom and her lover, and the housing project in Aberdare where vandals ruled and dog muck fouled the pavements. He would be going home to a life in a decaying industrial nation, closed-down coal mines and acid rain and small chance of getting employment. He would be selling his soul to the Department of Social Security for a weekly handout, and nothing to look forward to except premature balding and senile decay. It was not life Gareth would be returning to, but a kind of dying.

Desperate feelings churned in his stomach. He had come too far, and the Moon had changed him. Before, Pen-y-van had meant something to him. The gray mountains and the land of his fathers was the only place he knew. But now it meant nothing, offered nothing, and he did not want to go back there. There was no future for him on Earth and nothing he wanted. It was a world run by lunatics, and he would be trapped on it forever, like Bethkahn on the Moon, and unable to escape.

Suddenly Gareth knew how she felt, her screams echoing in his mind through ten thousand years of isolation. And he, with the mad world waiting, felt his own scream rising inside him. Go back to Earth and he would never be free again. There was agony inside him, despair black and destroying. He was sick with it, cold with it, and there was no way out.

"Is something the matter?" Karen asked him.

He looked at her, wildness in his eyes.

"I don't want to go!" he said. "There's nothing there! Nothing on Earth! Nowhere, not for me!"

"You can come to Santa Barbara," Karen said generously.

"What's the point?"

"Pop will find you a job."

"You don't understand!" wailed Gareth. "There's nothing *anywhere*! No reason! No purpose! Worth it for you, it is, but not for me! There's no meaning on Earth! Here's where the meaning began. Here! I want to go on, not back! For crying out loud—there's not even any hope!"

Karen stared at him. She wanted to help him, but she did not know how and she never would, nor did she begin to understand. Life was different for her. She still cared about having and getting, but he only cared about being. He did not belong on that teeming, struggling planet. He did not belong in Karen's world of backyard swimming pools and beach houses. She reached out to touch him, but Gareth pushed back his chair and walked away.

22

Karen was packing her bags and had no need of his company, so Gareth left the camera on the bed for her to find, picked up the bag containing the broken stabilizer, pocketed Graham Sanderson's knife, and headed away down the long corridor. He ignored the arrow that pointed the way to Medical. Accidentally and on purpose he had decided to forget the interview with Drew. This was his last day on the Moon, and he intended to use it. He would see Bethkahn's stabilizer mended and returned to her if it was the last thing he ever did.

His lips set in an obdurate line, and determination drove him. He passed a group of scientists by the elevator, but no one stopped or questioned him, and security guards in the nearby checkpoint paid him no heed. Gareth's expression was enough to tell them he knew exactly where he was going and for what purpose.

Double doors to the Vehicle Maintenance Department opened automatically and allowed him inside. The room was vast, filled with noise and bustle and pop music playing. Naked light bulbs hung from steel girders, and overhead skylights let in a little natural light. But shadows were predominant, areas of gloom and darkness, and coldness exuded from the concrete walls and floor. Garage smells assailed him—the reek of oil and sweat, greased machinery and dirty overalls. He heard the clatter of wrenches and the scream of a saw cutting through metal. A buggy stripped of its side panels showed a maze of multicolored wires, and another was suspended over a pit with a team of mechanics working under it. Unnoticeable among the noise and chaos, Gareth watched in bewilderment, his mind gone blank. But then among the sounds he heard the hiss of a welder and saw in the dark distance of the room a shower of sparks, and made his way toward it.

"Excuse me!" Gareth shouted.

A man in navy overalls turned toward him, his face lost among the reflections in his protective headgear. Lifting his visor, Graham Sanderson smiled.

"Hi Gareth. What can I do for you?"

"Your knife," said Gareth, and held it toward him.

He could hardly believe his luck! He had known Graham Sanderson worked here but he had not known he was actually a welder. He stayed to watch, shielding his eyes from the glaring point of laser light, seeing the blue sparks flying. He said he had always wanted to try his hand at welding, that he might even like to take it up professionally, and soon he was dressed in a greasy white boiler suit and extra headgear, listening and learning, attempting to grasp the basics. Under Graham Sanderson's guidance Gareth reinforced a fuel injection pipe without much trouble.

"Try something of my own, can I?" he asked. "Use that spare welder over there? I won't get in your way."

It was a souvenir from Surveyor Four that Gareth produced from the bag. He had picked it up in the Sinus Medii, he said, and he wanted to weld together the broken pieces and take it back to Earth. Graham Sanderson examined it curiously. It appeared to be some kind of rotor with two of its blades sheared off. Its function puzzled him, nor did he recognize the metal. It was an alloy he had never come across before. Other men gathered around, and Gareth started to sweat.

"Where did you say it came from?" one of them asked.

"Surveyor Four," said Gareth.

"It's damned odd," said another.

"But can it be mended?" Gareth asked anxiously.

Initially, to the men of the Vehicle Maintenance Department, it was regarded as a curio, a temporary distraction that challenged their powers of deduction during the official coffee break. They discovered that the metal was heat resistant, unaffected except by the hottest temperature. White heat melted it, but theoretically it was capable of withstanding reentry into the Earth's atmosphere, and they could not understand why it had been taken out of production. They could only assume it was discarded for its brittle qualities, its proneness to fracturing.

"But can it be mended?" Gareth repeated.

"It's a three-hour job," said one of the men.

"I've got nothing else to do," Gareth assured them.

"It would take an expert, son."

"If you'll just show me how to start . . ."

Gareth was surrounded by experts. Among the blast of a rivet gun, the fine whine of a drill, and machine tools singing all around him, he watched as the pieces of stabilizer were clamped in a vise and saw the laser light spark. Gobbets of hot metal fell to the floor, liquefied like mercury. It was not easy. When Gareth took over he was awkward and incompetent. The men had to take it in turns, leaving their own work to spend time with him, instructing him, advising him, showing him how. And Gareth was always willing to stand aside and admire their expertise.

To the men of the Vehicle Maintenance Department he was grateful in more ways than one—glad of their company and lunch in the snack bar, the noise and music and shouted conversations that gave him no chance to brood. It was time being utilized for a purpose, and it was midafternoon when Gareth left. The stabilizer hung heavy and solid in the gray bag over his shoulder. It was as strong as it had ever been, Graham Sanderson said. Strong enough to withstand the takeoff of Beth-kahn's starship, Gareth thought, and there was a kind of joy in knowing that. She would have a future now, freedom to travel and something to hope for. But depression gripped him when he thought of himself.

He did not have any hope. He would be returning to Earth. Trapped in a prison of flesh he would serve out his sentence, his life continuing as it had before . . . inescapable . . . unless . . . ? A huge fear touched him, and he cut off the thought, and there were voices drifting through the open rectangle of a nearby doorway— his doorway. Drew and Karen were inside his room! Gareth stopped walking, thought to hide in the bathroom, but they saw him and so he walked on. They were blue-gray shapes in the gloomy light of the Moon's sunset, distant beings in another reality. He was remote from them and unrelated. And something had ended hours ago between himself and Karen.

"Been poking in my room, have you?"

"I was looking for my camera," Karen said.

"And where have *you* been?" Drew asked him.

"Vehicle Maintenance," Gareth said.

"We were supposed to be meeting for lunch!" Karen said sourly.

"I had lunch in the snack bar," Gareth said.

"Open your bag," said Drew.

"What?"

"Open it!"

"What *is* this?"

"Drew wants the sphere," said Karen.

Gareth swallowed, unfastened the straps of Bethkahn's shoulder bag, and showed Drew the stabilizer. It had come from the Vehicle Maintenance Department, he said angrily, and he had spent all morning welding it together, for something to do. If Drew wanted the sphere he should have looked in the closet, on the shelf.

"We *have* looked in the closet," Karen said. "We've looked everywhere. We've even checked the toilet tanks in the bathroom."

"So where is it?" asked Drew. "You had it last night in the plastic shopping bag. What have you done with it?"

"It's in the flaming closet!" Gareth said savagely. "I flaming put it there! I tried to give it to the security guards, but they wouldn't listen!" He flung open the closet door, allowed a few seconds to register apparent shock before the contrived reaction. "Flaming hell! It's gone!"

Karen turned to Drew.

Her voice was shrill.

"What did I tell you? If Gareth hasn't taken it then who has? It's *got* to be her!"

"Let's not jump to conclusions," Drew said quickly.

"What's she talking about?" Gareth asked.

"The girl!" shrilled Karen. "The one you saw in the dust storm when Charlie Kunik died! The one from the alien spaceship! She *did* come here last night! She came to your room, Gary, and took back the sphere!"

"Don't talk stupid! I would have seen her!"

"You didn't see anything!" Karen said wildly. "You were asleep! You never heard the second alarm siren! You never heard me come to your room! She could have killed you, and you wouldn't have known!"

Gareth shrugged.

"That's one explanation, I suppose. And what's gone is gone. Now if you don't mind I've got some packing to do."

Quite deliberately Gareth did not look at Drew or Karen. He dragged out his travel bag and closed the closet door. Then he tipped his clothes onto the bed and started to fold them, shirts and sweatshirts, smoothing the creases. Karen started to say something but decided not to, and a moment later Gareth heard the door close behind him. He thought they had gone but when he turned his head Drew was standing there.

"Why didn't you show me the sphere?"

"Because I didn't know what it was."

"Karen says it was a robotic spying device."

"That's only a theory."

"And what about this girl you claimed to have seen?"

"What about her?"

"Jake says he saw her, too."

Gareth bit his lip.

"Is Jake all right?" he asked.

"He will be, providing he can come to terms with the experience," said Drew. "For his sake I have to ask you—was she real? *Is* she real? Is this what we're up against, an alien life form? Is this what I should advise the base commander? This time I take you seriously, Gareth!"

Hunkered on his heels Gareth stayed still. He did not know what to say, how to answer, or how to protect Bethkahn. Truth or lies? Whatever he said Drew was ready to believe him, and Drew was no fool. He was a trained psychologist. One slip of the tongue, one thoughtless mistake, and Drew would be onto it. For Gareth's own sake, as well as for Jake, he had to play safe.

"Last night," said Gareth. "When I came back from the bathroom the security guards were searching. What did they find?"

"Nothing," Drew said evenly.

"What did they hope to find?"

Drew sighed.

"Okay," he said. "I guess I can level with you. That dust storm we encountered on the day Charlie Kunik died was not a straightforward phenomenon. From satellite recordings our computers picked up a faint heat-trace reading, a moving point of energy at the epicenter of the storm. I'm not saying this is evidence and proves you were right, but when the second dust storm happened, and Jake's garbled account told a similar story, it seemed prudent to order a full-scale search. I'm not sure what we expected to find—something or nothing—but we were obligated to check."

"And as it happened you found nothing," Gareth said quietly. "But something, it seems, came here to my room and took the sphere from my closet. So what does that suggest to you, Drew?"

Anxiety showed in Drew's eyes.

"I'll see you later," he said.

23

Gareth stared through the window at the disk of the sun sinking infinitely slowly behind the Lunar Apennines. Nightlong the rim of Mount Conon would eat it away, and before the dawn darkness Bethkahn would return. He had less than twelve hours to make up his mind—whether to go back to Earth or go with her, and both ways he had to be desperate. It was one thing believing he was more than flesh and blood, that there was another side to him indestructible and immortal, but he was not dying to prove it, no more than he was dying to return to Earth. Faced with the choice between life and death Gareth could not decide which he feared most. Drew nudged him, pointed to the steak pie and mashed potatoes on the plate.

"Your food's growing cold."

"What I need is food for my soul," Gareth muttered.

"That's a very peculiar remark," said Drew.

"He's been peculiar all day," Karen said sourly.

"Man shall not live by bread alone," Gareth quoted.

"So what brought this on?" Drew asked.

"Better eat up," J.B. told him. "Russian hospitality is not like ours. All you'll get in the Sinus Iridum is black bread and water."

Gareth scowled at his plate.

"Steak pie or black bread, it's all the same—gut fodder! But there is another deeper hunger that cannot be satisfied, see?"

"Ah," said Drew. "I'm beginning to see."

"I meant to tell you this morning," said J.B.

"How serious is this?" asked Drew.

"He doesn't want to go back," said Karen.

"Nor would you if you had to face my prospects!" Gareth retorted.

"You don't have to go back to Wales," Karen told him. "I've invited you to come to Santa Barbara. Pop will find you a job."

"There you are," J.B. said cheerfully. "The world is your oyster, son. Work hard, save your dollars, invest wisely. You'll be a millionaire by the time you're thirty."

"What good's that?" Gareth said viciously. "The only purpose of money is to buy *things*. Why should I spend the rest of my life scrimping and saving to buy a load of blasted cars and washing machines and a thousand and one consumer goods that I could do without? What a flaming waste of life! There's got to be more than that. There's got to be!"

"Life gets better as you get older," J.B. assured him.

"Not in Aberdare!"

"Even in Aberdare," said Drew. "You can take my word for it. You'll find a meaning."

But words did not help. What was true for Drew and the base commander might not be true for Gareth. He saw things differently, and all he had to go on were his own experiences. They had probably bred, Bethkahn had said of the beings who had once shared her starship, and Gareth was the result. He had a body evolved from the beasts of the Earth, a soul evolved from the stars. He inherited the conflict, torn between spirit and flesh, between Earth's bleak reality and Bethkahn's universe, fear and faith. But the fear was stronger, sheer physicality holding him back, temptation in a dish of lemon sherbet. On Bethkahn's starship, robotic waiters served amber wine in tall glasses. Sensations were not dimmed, she had said, and taste was just as sweet. But words could be lies, and there was only one way for Gareth to find out. Gloomily he picked up the spoon . . . and what he ate was synthetic junk.

"Shall we go for a last swim in the pool?" asked Karen.

"And a last Coke in the moonbase bar?" suggested Drew.

"*You* can," said Gareth. "I'm going to bed."

Karen sighed.

"Do you have to be miserable on our last night?"

"I think you should make an effort," said Drew.

"You have to snap out of it, son," J.B. said kindly.

"Please, Gary, let's have a farewell party," Karen said.

"And here come the guests of honor," said J.B.

White and red, the Russian hopper set down on the landing pad outside, sank and settled in a swirl of dust, looking like a bowlegged beetle with porthole windows along the side, the size of a double-decker bus. The base commander buttoned his Air Force jacket and hurried to greet the Soviet team. Gareth went swimming. And afterward he went to the moonbase bar to join the party. He went because Drew was watching him—gray eyes, with a degree in psychology behind them, summing him up, his dour silence and symptoms of depression. He knew if he was not careful he would end up being analyzed, or drugged into quiescence, dosed with sleeping pills for a night when he needed to stay awake. Ice chinked in his glass, and he fixed a smile on his face.

The room seemed overrun by Russians in gray uniforms, the big promotion scene for East-West relations, handshakes and introductions and background music giving an air of gaiety that was totally false. It was like holding a wake before the funeral, and Gareth was part of it, laughing and talking and playing at being himself—bones and a body with his name attached.

"Mikhail Denovitch," J.B. boomed. "Meet our young visitors. This is Karen. And this is Gareth—the first Welshman on the Moon. If daffodils bloom next spring in the Mare Vaporum it'll be his doing. And you've heard about the bones of the moon beast, of course."

The Russian smiled.

"You are the joker, Gareth?"

"Not tonight," said Karen. "Tonight he's pretending he's not one hundred percent miserable."

"You are not drinking the bourbon," Mikhail Denovitch said. "I buy you one, eh?"

"Go on," said Drew. "Have one to drown your sorrows."

"What I need is a permanent solution," said Gareth. "Not a temporary escape route and a thick head. How about a job at the Russian base? Fully qualified, I am. Clean your boots or polish your buggies. Good for nothing, see, with first-class references."

The Russian laughed.

And the base commander's paternal hand rested on Gareth's shoulder. "We're sure going to miss this guy," he said.

But when Gareth slipped away half an hour later no one missed him. Drew was too busy chatting with Valerie Doyle from Communications to notice, and Karen was teaching Mikhail Denovitch to dance. Down empty corridors Gareth walked, and the bright electric lights did not dispel his mood of gloom. And the bare white room with its packed travel bag, closed door, and dull sunset light enhanced it. He felt isolated from everyone, and his sense of unbelonging grew to a kind of terror. The Lunacy Syndrome had its dark side, Drew had said, and solitude was dangerous. What the stars had begun in the first moment of the Moon's morning was now complete. Gareth was meaningless. His stay

168

at the moonbase was over, and on Earth, among the teeming billions of people, his absence would be no loss. Who he was and what he did mattered to no one but himself.

He stood staring out at the darkening landscape, the desert of gray-brown dust and tumbled ridges where nothing lived or moved—only an alien girl who watched and waited, Bethkahn with her amber eyes and drifts of dark hair. He mattered to her. She thought of him and wished for him, not caring about his past or future. She had not said so, but he had felt it, a need in her as deep as his own, her loneliness touching him in the silence. She had not needed to ask why he would help her; that he did was an answer in itself. And he had not needed to ask her what life was like on Khio Three because she too was an answer. She represented it—a beautiful being from a beautiful world. He knew now why men looked up at the stars and called them heaven. A part of them remembered, paradise echoing through generations of human dreams. And Bethkahn with her starship could take him back there, to the land of his fathers that had never been Wales.

Nine thousand light-years, Bethkahn had said.

He would be dead before he got there.

And that was the permanent solution, the final freedom.

But Gareth was convinced he was not just physical.

Like Bethkahn he had an astral body.

The Moon had proved it.

The *Zen Buddhist's Handbook* confirmed it.

Yet the fear remained.

He was afraid of knowing, afraid of extinction, afraid of nothing . . . scared out of his mind. "Help me!" he whispered. But no one came. It was his decision. His and his alone.

Later, as Gareth lay unsleeping fully clothed under the blanket, Drew looked in. Behind him in the lighted corridor Karen giggled and hiccuped and he hushed her to silence and closed the door. There was no sound then but the hum of the air-conditioning and the thud of Gareth's heart as he sat up and waited, watching as the line of light below his door faded at midnight, and the moonbase slept.

He was in no hurry. Time ticked by on his wristwatch, and the fear was gone. A strange calm gripped him, and his stockinged feet made no sound upon the floor tiles when he finally made his move. With the bag containing the stabilizer slung over his shoulder, Gareth opened the door, glanced left and right along the darkened corridor, then hurried away in the direction of the main reception area. Without his weighted training shoes his body felt light and floating, unreal and unbelonging and disconnected from his head. A murmur of voices drifted from the cafeteria, and the Communications room was bright with light, fully staffed, as Gareth went past. No one saw him. And when he turned the corner he waited in the shadows until the guards in the security checkpoint turned their backs, then slipped into the room where the space suits were kept.

There was no one on duty at that time of night—just

rows of silver suits, racks of helmets and oxygen cylinders and strap harnesses on hooks, toilet facilities in the unlit room beyond. Gareth had no plan, but his gaze fixed immediately on the Russian helmets, scarlet and white and bearing the symbols of the Soviet Union. Even from a distance they were unmistakable, quite distinct from the helmets used by the Americans. A few words of Welsh mistaken for Russian, and Gareth would be away. He dressed hurriedly and locked himself in a toilet stall to wait for Bethkahn's approach.

He had to see her again. He had to talk to her. He did not have long to wait—maybe half an hour of sweating inside the insulated suit before the alarm sirens wailed. Then he acted—fitted the oxygen cylinder, buckled the harness, and sealed the Russian helmet. Wrist dials showed green as he picked up the bag and reentered the corridor.

Just as last night, the moonbase was in panic, lights going on and armed guards running in all directions. It was a weird feeling—seeing but not hearing, a goldfish in a bowl staring through the glass at an alien world in which he could not live, could not belong. He felt like a ghost, sitting inside himself and looking out, uninvolved with what went on, not caring about their hopes and fears or the planet they came from. For seventeen years he had been acting out a role in their ghastly pantomime, but now it was over . . . almost.

Gesticulating wildly Gareth approached the checkpoint, a Russian gabbling in some unintelligible language across the suit's transmitter, adding to the general confusion. The two security guards barring his way to the air lock stared at him in alarm. Gareth opened the bag, pointed to the stabilizer and then to the air lock, allowed himself to speak a few words of broken English.

"This," he said. "Into hopper. I go quick."

"You've got to be mad going out there, buddy."

"Orders," said Gareth. "Mikhail Denovitch."

"Okay screwball—it's your life."

"I go?" Gareth said urgently.

"Sure," said the guard. "Carry on."

Gareth did not hesitate. The doors closed behind him. Wall dials in the outer chamber showed zero pressure, and then he was outside. He saw the hopper squatting on the landing pad. He saw the desert stretching out before him, empty, unreal, no one on it. Men would never reach the Moon, never set their feet upon the dust or breathe in the airless spaces. The Moon was a dream, the orbed maiden out of myth and poetry, ruthless and lonely, waiting to kill. But Gareth rounded the corner, crossed the concrete of the loading bay, and went to meet her. Stars blazed, and the sun was half gone behind the rim of Mount Conon. Dust blew in the wind. He thought of peppermint gum and Drew's red hair. He thought of Jake singing, Mom and her lover, and the dull gray streets of Aberdare. But his voice was a cry of joy in the moonwind rising.

"I'm here, Bethkahn!"

24

Karen stood in the reception area in the long, empty minutes before departure. It was dark outside, the shadowy landscape stretching away, desolate below the stars. And the stars were more brilliant than she had ever seen them, gold and glorious in the black depths of space. Their beauty mocked her. They made her feel small and insignificant, without identity. She wanted to go home, back to America where she knew who she was—Karen Angers, her mother's daughter, her kid brother's sister, a pupil at Santa Barbara High School and dating Joey Bellini on Saturday nights. She was meaningless on the Moon. It was lethal and lonely, nothing to do with "Phoebe Unveiled," the imagery of poetry and the essay that had brought her here. More like it was the "Lunacy Syndrome" come to life, a hideous madness. Slow tears trickled down her face as she thought of him. His name was Gareth. It had always been Gareth, and she wanted to scream at him in anger and despair, demand an answer . . . for Pete's sake why? But Gareth was dead, and the hopper was twelve hours late in leaving, and all she could do was cry.

Drew brought her bags.

"They're taking him out now," he said.

The arc lamps switched on, showing the Russian hopper standing on the landing pad, its air lock doors open to receive its passengers. Karen covered her face with her hands. She did not want to see—two corpses sewn in their canvas shrouds, and one of them Gareth. Great sobs shook her body, and Drew held her, smoothing her hair.

"Why did he do it?" Karen wept. "Why did he go outside? He knew what she was—ruthless and lonely. He knew she killed Charlie Kunik, so why did he go? How could he be so stupid?" Drew did not answer, but his touch went on, soothing, comforting, and the words poured from her. "She wasn't even human, so what did he want from her? What did he hope for? He could have come with me to Santa Barbara, but he turned to her, and she murdered him. She *murdered* him, Drew!"

"No," said Drew. "That's not what happened. We have no real proof of this girl's existence and no evidence to suggest that anyone other than Gareth released the seals on his helmet. He died by his own hand, Karen, while the balance of his mind—"

"No! He wouldn't do that! *She* killed him!"

"I think you should face it, sweetheart."

"No! I won't believe it!"

"Listen to me. Listen Karen. Gareth was depressed. He made it quite clear he didn't want to return to Earth. If you have to blame someone then blame me. His death was my fault. I should have realized . . ."

Drew's voice trailed away, and Karen raised her head to look at him. His face was pale beneath the red thatch of his hair, and his gray eyes looked stricken. On a personal level Drew was as much in need of comfort as she was.

"Why should I blame you?" Karen said wretchedly. "He knew what could happen. He was probably trying to hitch a ride on her spaceship. That's the sort of stupid thing he'd try for! I could believe that! But I can't believe in suicide. That's the coward's way out, and Gareth wasn't a coward!"

"No," said Drew. "He was never that."

"So what possible reason could he have had?"

"The permanent solution?" said Drew.

Karen sat heavily on the red padded bench. She could not take it in, could not accept it. She could not wait to get back to Earth, yet Drew said Gareth had died rather than return there, deliberately killed himself. It could not be true! But there was no place on Earth for him, he had said, no reason or purpose working all his life for a load of things he did not want. Suddenly, clear and terrible, Karen saw the world through Gareth's eyes in everything he had talked of—the cruelty and injustice, the squalid streets of Aberdare, his mother living with a man he had not liked. It was all right for

Karen living on the rich West Coast of America. She could remain untouched by it all. But Gareth had despised wealth as much as he had despised poverty. He had turned down the opportunities she had offered because he could not close his eyes to things, could never forgive or forget.

Understanding, Karen hung her head. Gold bangles jangling on her wrists shamed her. She had thought herself lucky to be born American, but now she was ashamed of it, and the tears she cried were different tears, galling, humiliating, guilt mixed with grief. The Moon changed everyone. Gareth had died, and Karen would never be the same again.

"What are we doing?" she sobbed. "What are we thinking of? It's all gone wrong. The whole world's gone wrong. We spend billions of dollars on a useless moonbase, billions more on weapons of destruction, on stupid fashions and cosmetic surgery and so many worthless things. We spend, and others starve, and Gareth could not bear to go back to that. I know how he felt, but he didn't have to die because of it. He could have stayed and fought! He could have fought it much better than me! He could have done so much, and now he can do nothing! So what was the point of it?"

Drew sighed.

"I suppose he saw it as the only way out."

"But he was so alive!" said Karen. "He was the most alive person I ever met. Maddening and infuriating and enough to drive anyone crazy, but he seemed to give out a kind of life. The Moon wasn't dead while he was on it—it was full of bones and daffodils, and pickle factories, silly, ridiculous things. He fooled us, Drew. He was always fooling us. He wouldn't give that up!"

Drew shrugged.

"Maybe he fooled himself," he said bleakly.

"Maybe," Karen said doubtfully. "I know he believed it. He believed in astral bodies and alien spaceships. He believed in the girl too. He believed so much he made me believe also. Why would he believe it if there was no truth in it? Why would he?"

"I think," said Drew, "that we will never know."

"Do you know what I think?" Karen asked. "I think there's something we're not seeing—that he raised his finger to the whole goddam world and is laughing at us."

"Which doesn't alter the fact." Drew sighed.

Karen echoed his sigh, turned to watch the hopper being loaded—an enemy machine, red and white with its symbols of Soviet power. In their silver suits the men worked together, Russian and American, indistinguishable one from another except for their helmets. They were all human beings, all the same underneath.

"I wish I understood," Karen muttered. "I wouldn't mind so much if I knew the reason. It's wasting everything Gareth was, and it just doesn't fit."

Karen leaped to her feet.

The men outside ran for cover.

And a moment later the siren sounded.

"It's another dust storm!" Drew said anxiously.

"No," said Karen. "Look over there! It's that volcano! It's an eruption!"

The sky above the Lunar Apennines pulsed red and golden with light and fire. Mount Conon was alive, belching smoke and dust and clouding the stars. But then, in the heart of it, something moved—a vast silver shape among the detritus.

Slowly and ponderously the starship rose, lifting above the crater rim as the siren wailed and moonbase personnel came running and crowding around the windows, their voices shrill with fear and disbelief.

"Is that what I think it is?"

"Some kind of joke?"

"No joke, buddy, it's a flying saucer!"

"It's not true! It can't be!"

"God almighty! Will you look at the size of it!"

"I reckon we've had it! I reckon we don't stand a chance!"

"We're sitting ducks!"

"Someone inform the base commander!"

"We need a nuclear strike, immediately!"

"It's too damned close! We'd be blown to pieces!"

"Lord, into thy hands . . ."

Karen stared at the ship in terror, felt Drew's arm tighten around her. He had not been able to believe what Gareth had said, but everyone believed it now. It was there before them—an alien spaceship hovering hugely above the mountains, then veering toward them. Green, red, blue, yellow, and purple, it flashed its multitude of colored lights as its great bulk sailed across the stars and slowly approached. It hung there, motionless, just a few hundred feet up, seeming to fill the whole sky. The siren ceased, and the lights flashed off and on in the long, terrible seconds of silence. They were waiting to die, spellbound people holding their breaths. But the ship did not kill. Beautiful and spectacular as in a fairy-tale city in space, the colored lights flickered off and on, off and on, as if the starship signaled.

"Screw me!" someone said. "It's moonbase morse!"

Someone else laughed nervously.

"Don't be ridiculous! How the hell would a flying saucer know moonbase morse?"

"By tapping our computers," a security guard said grimly.

"I think it's just random signaling," said Valerie Doyle from Communications. "Gobbledygook. No . . . es . . . da . . . car . . . I . . . ad . . . No . . . es . . . It just keeps repeating it, words with no sense attached. Nos . . . da . . . car-I-ad. Some foreign language perhaps?"

Karen stared at the sky, at the colored lights flashing off and on, off and on. *Nos da, cariad. Nos da.* The colors whispered deep in her mind, glorious with meaning. Gareth had fooled them, just as she had said. Wild with joy, Karen pushed past the security guard and hurled herself at the window. Two hands waved back at him and her voice was screaming.

"*Nos da*, Gareth! *Nos da!*"

179

"Karen?" said Drew. "What do you think you're doing?"
She turned toward him.

Her eyes were shining in the light.

"It's Welsh," she said. "Good night, darling. *Nos da, cariad*. That's what it means."

"We've no Welsh in our computers," someone said.

"No," said Karen. "But Gareth knows it. He's up there! Saying good-bye . . . to me."

"It's coincidence," said Valerie Doyle.

"Gareth is dead," said Drew.

But Karen would not listen, did not care. She turned back to the window. Click-flash . . . Someone beside her was using her camera, taking pictures of the ship, and the movie camera whirred. But Karen had her memory and would never forget—magical colors, blue, red, yellow, purple, and green, speaking for Gareth, letting her know. He had to go on, not back. The Moon had changed him, and this was the meaning he had talked of—life itself. It was more than the color of a skin, the needs of a body, the wants and greeds of Earth. He had believed it, trusted it, the permanent solution—life, not death. Deep inside herself Karen felt the stirring of her own immortal existence, a surge of power and her soul leaping in joy as she became aware of it. For a trip on a starship and an alien girl Gareth had died and lived, but he had not forgotten Karen. *"Nos da, cariad."* The colors whispered and moondust swirled in the wind as the great ship lifted upward.

"Gee, it's fantastic!" Karen said.

And laughed through her tears.